A CALLAHAN WEDDING

A CALLAHAN WEDDING

MONICA MURPHY

Cover design: Enchanting Book Designs

Editor: Rebecca, Fairest Reviews Editing Services
Proofreader: Sarah, All Encompassing Books

CHAPTER 1

HANNAH

"*Y*ou seem stressed."

I glance up, resting my fork on my plate. I've been picking at my food for the last fifteen minutes. Jake Callahan—star NFL quarterback, love of my life, my future husband—is sitting across from me at the table, watching me carefully. His dark brows are drawn together, his mouth turned down in a frown.

It's November. The football season is in full swing, and his team has a good chance at making the playoffs, even though it's early days still and Jake hates it when I make predictions this soon. He claims I'm going to jinx them.

I can't help it if I have complete confidence in his abilities.

"I'm not stressed." The lie falls from my lips automatically, as if I have no control over myself. I don't want to stress him out with my problems. He's got enough to deal with. I told myself I could handle the wedding planning, but oh my God.

It's...

It's a lot.

"Hannah," he reaches across the table, his fingers curling around mine, "come on. Out with it."

We're at a quiet restaurant on a Tuesday night, one that's not too far from where we live in Phoenix. Most people who come here ignore the fact that Jake is a celebrity, which he appreciates. That's why we come here so often.

He's going out of town for an away game later this week, and I'm not able to go with him because I'm preparing for a new art showing that's happening next spring, which means I'm painting long into the night, almost every night. I need enough work to show in the gallery, and it takes months to prepare for something like this.

I'm living my dream as an artist. I'm living with my husband-to-be, whose career is going nowhere but up. Same with mine. I should be feeling on top of the world.

Instead, I'm on the verge of tears.

Taking a deep breath, I let it all out. "The wedding planning isn't going well."

His frown deepens. "What do you mean?"

"We can't find a venue. Not one big enough." I press my lips together, willing myself not to cry.

"What do you mean, not big enough? I thought we agreed our wedding was going to be on the smaller side?" He looks confused, which I suppose he is. So much has happened in the last few months, and I thought I had it under control, but clearly, I don't.

"Everything sort of blew up," I admit. "And when I say everything, I mean our invitation list."

He squints at me, as if he's trying to see inside my head, which is the last place I want him to see. It's pure chaos in there. "How many people are you wanting to invite?"

"It's not me wanting to invite them, it's everyone who wants an invite," I clarify. "And the list is up to—"

Oh God, I don't want to say it out loud.

"Up to what?" he asks when I still haven't said.

"Six hundred," I whisper.

His eyes look like they're going to bug out of his head. "Six hundred? Did I hear you right?"

I shrug one shoulder, reaching for my wine glass, so I can take a fortifying sip. I think I need liquid courage for this conversation. "There are so many people to consider. Our friends, our families. Everyone on your team and whoever their plus one is. Then there are my new friends here. Media people who you've become close to."

I could go on and on. I don't know how to say no. Once people found out we were getting married, the requests to attend started pouring in from people we don't even know that well. It's wild, how many people want to come to our wedding, but Jake is a celebrity, so I suppose I get it.

"That's too many people, Hannah. Our wedding should be just for us and our friends and family," he says, his voice gentle. I think he can tell I'm barely hanging on as it is right now. He doesn't want to push me over that edge. "Don't you agree?"

"I do, it's just...I don't want to turn people down, Jake. Most of those who want to come to our wedding, we know."

"And then there are people we don't know who want to come," he points out. He squeezes my hand, and when I try to pull away, he won't let me. "I don't want this to turn into a circus."

"I don't either," I agree, offering him a weak smile. "Plus, it's going to be so expensive."

"Money isn't an issue," he says with a finality that tells me he doesn't want an argument. "Maybe we should just run away."

It's my turn to frown. "What are you talking about?"

"Go to some tropical island with the family and get married. Have our wedding and honeymoon all at once. What do you think?"

I love how that sounds, but I shake my head. "We can't.

3

I've already put down deposits on the flowers and the caterer."

"Even though you haven't found the spot where our reception is going to be?" He lets go of my hand and grabs his water glass, downing almost half of it. Pretty sure he's as stressed as I am now. "You shouldn't have to deal with this. I thought that was why we hired the wedding planner."

"It is. Cindy is great." She is. She has great ideas and she's busting her butt trying to find a venue for our potentially massive reception. "It's just that our wedding planning has been so last minute. There's not a lot available out there."

"I bet Hawaii is nice in March." Jake smirks.

"March? Our wedding is planned for April."

"Nothing is set in stone. We haven't sent out invitations yet."

Cindy really wanted us to send out save the date cards, but we didn't. Anyone who is important to us will be there. We don't need to send them a postcard, letting them know when we're getting married. At least, that's what Jake said.

Such a man, my fiancé.

"I don't know…" My voice drifts, and I drop my gaze to my hands, and the giant diamond on my ring finger. I remember when he gave it to me. How nervous he looked when he got down on one knee and took my hand in his. The sincerity burning bright in his blue eyes as he stared up at me and asked that one question that changed our lives forever.

Will you marry me?

When the man you love finally asks you to marry him, you say yes. And I did, without any hesitation. That was the moment I'd been waiting for, and once he asked, we wasted no time. We want to get married right away.

Even though it's proving a little difficult, which is mostly why I'm stressed.

Jake and I have been together a long time now. Since our

senior year in high school, when he would come over to my apartment and hang out with me while my mom was working the graveyard shift. He claimed he worried about my safety, but I don't know.

I think he really just wanted to spend time with me.

I wrote him off as an egotistical jock back then, but there's more to Jake than that. He's sweet and caring. Always thinking about me and including me in every aspect of his life. He's sensitive and so incredibly smart. He knows how to let loose and have fun, yet understands when he needs to be serious too. He has a good sense of humor, and he's such a loyal friend. He loves his family. He loves football and is a terrific leader, no matter which team he's with.

And he loves me.

I can see all that love right now, written all over his face. He's worried about me, and I love that. How much he cares. How much he sees.

I've become friends with some of the women whose boyfriends/husbands play for the team, and some of them complain about how they don't come first. That their man ignores them, or only talks about himself. Some of them are worried that he's cheating. The fame and the women and the attention gets to some of those football players, and it goes to their heads.

Not Jake. He grew up with it because of his father. He saw what it was like, and lived that life as the first son of an NFL superstar. Now he's one as well and it doesn't seem to get to him like the others. He's not out messing around or drinking too much, or behaving recklessly. I'm secure in the fact that I'm the most important thing to him. Even above football.

And that says a lot.

"Consider it," he says, when I haven't said anything else. "Running away and getting married on a tropical island could be fun."

"But what about—"

"I don't care about anyone else," he interrupts, glancing around to make sure no one in the restaurant is paying attention to us. Thankfully, no one is. "I only care about you. And me. Our family and friends. But hell, if it was just the two of us running away to get married, I'd be okay with that. I love you, Hannah. I don't need to have a flashy wedding reception to tell everyone that. I just want you."

My heart threatens to burst at his words. How does he do this? Just…come up with the absolute best things to say to make me melt? "I love you too. But—give me a little more time to see if I can make this happen, okay? Cindy is working so hard for us, trying to find a suitable location. I'd hate to have to tell her to stop."

"You're not doing this to make Cindy, the wedding planner, happy," Jake reminds me. "We're doing this to make each other happy. Remember that."

His words run through my mind once we return home. When he drags me into the bedroom, his touch insistent, his mouth seeking and finding mine when he's got me pressed against the wall in our room. He devours me, his hand sneaking beneath my dress, fingers dancing along my thigh as they move up, up…

Until they're diving beneath my panties, his breath hot against my lips as he begins to stroke.

"Nothing else matters," he whispers as his fingers bring me to orgasm. "Only you. And me."

I circle my arms around his neck, clinging to him when he makes me come. Sometimes I marvel at the fact that this man chose me, over everyone else. I don't have these thoughts as much as I used to, but every once in a while, it hits me.

When I was younger, I used to think I was no one special. Downright invisible. Until Jake Callahan set his gaze on me and never let up. He pursued me with an intensity I couldn't help but find attractive. He wanted me. Nothing was going to stop him.

And it felt good to be wanted. It still does.

The man doesn't define me, but he's encouraged me from the very beginning to be my own person. He lifts me up, and I try my hardest to do the same for him. We make a good team. I'm lucky to be loved by this man, and I know he feels the same way about me.

The moment my shivering subsides, he's picking me up, carrying me over to our bed and dropping me onto the mattress, making me laugh. I watch as he strips out of his clothes, revealing his muscular chest. His long, muscular legs. His erection strains against the front of his navy boxer briefs and everything inside me flutters in anticipation.

Jake Callahan still gives me butterflies.

He catches me staring and wraps his fingers around his cotton-covered dick, giving himself a teasing stroke. "You want it?"

Such a silly question. Of course, I want it.

I nod, not saying a word.

"Take off your dress." He flicks his chin at me.

I do as he says, shedding the dress in seconds and dropping it onto the floor.

"Your bra."

Reaching behind me, I undo the snap and get rid of my bra.

"Lean back." An almost feral gleam shines in his eyes and I know what he wants before he even says it. "Touch yourself."

I'm about to shed my panties when his deep voice stops me. "Keep 'em on."

Locking my gaze with his, I slip my fingers beneath the front of my panties and touch myself, all the air gathering in my throat when I encounter nothing but wetness. I'm soaked for him, thanks to that earlier orgasm, and I can tell he's enjoying watching me play with myself, my fingers moving beneath the stretched fabric of my panties.

Jake states the obvious.

"You're wet."

So wet, I can hear it. He can too.

He gets rid of his boxer briefs, and my gaze zeroes in on his thick cock. Even when we're at our busiest, we always make time for each other. Most of our family and friends all have children, but we don't. I don't think we're even close to wanting them yet. There's still so much to do, and it's difficult to do those things when you're also taking care of a family. I want children with Jake—he's going to make a terrific father someday—but not yet.

I'm perfectly content with just the two of us. I love Jake's nieces and nephews, but it is so nice to hand them over at the end of the day and not have to worry about them any longer.

Someday, I think to myself as Jake joins me on the bed, his large, warm body hovering over mine. Someday, we'll make babies. But for now…

We're still in practice mode.

CHAPTER 2

JAKE

"Tell us about the wedding plans."

This comes from my little sister Ava, who's sitting across from Hannah and me, her husband Eli by her side. We went out to dinner after a football game where Eli and I played against each other—and damn it, we lost.

While Eli Bennett has come a long way from the ultra-competitive, taunting son of a bitch he used to be when he played QB for our biggest rival high school back in the day, he really hasn't changed a damn bit.

The moment he saw me after the game, he rubbed it in my face that he beat us, and I let him have his glory moment. He hasn't had too many of those when he's come up against me in the past.

Not bragging either. Just stating facts.

I send Hannah a quick look and see the exhaustion flit across her face at first mention of wedding plans. It's become a trigger word for her, swear to God.

"They're coming along," she says vaguely.

Eli rubs his hands together, his excitement palpable. "I

hear it's going to be a big shindig. I can't wait. It's going to be an epic party."

Where the hell did he hear that?

"Yeah, I guess," Hannah says, glancing over at me helplessly. "The guest list is huge."

Ava frowns. "How many people are you inviting?"

"Close to six hundred." Hannah winces.

"Isn't that ridiculous?" I ask Ava, who's frowning at me.

"Ridiculously awesome," Eli answers for his wife. "Like I said, epic party. We'll all be reunited. I haven't seen Caleb and Tony in so long."

"Don't forget Jackson," Ava says. "I miss Ellie so bad. I can't wait to see her."

Another helpless look from my future wife, her expression saying, *See? They are expecting this wedding to happen!*

Yeah, well we're not responsible for everyone's happiness.

"You got a DJ?" Eli asks.

"We need a DJ?" I glance over at Hannah. I mean, I know this. I've been to weddings before. But I've been wrapped up in my own shit and not really thinking about the wedding, unless Hannah asks me a question or needs my input.

Which makes me feel like shit. She's working too. She has a showing coming up and she's been in her studio, painting all day and sometimes even late into the night. She'll get so into it that she loses all track of time.

She tends to forget to call or text people back when she's like this—meaning the wedding planner. I'm sure that's not helping matters, but I can't hold it against her.

I love how passionate Hannah is about creating art. I love even more how successful she is. People respond to her work. Her paintings make people feel something, and that's so freaking cool.

I'm so proud of her. I don't say that enough. I need to tell her more often.

"We definitely need one," Hannah tells me, knocking me out of my thoughts. "And I found one—already put a deposit on that too."

"Planning a wedding is so stressful," Ava says, bringing up Hannah's fears. *Gee, thanks sis.* "I remember when I was putting ours together. All the stress made my face break out."

I check Hannah's profile and see nothing but smooth skin and the faintest freckles dotting her cheeks and the bridge of her nose. That must be a good sign.

"And it's so expensive," Ava continues. "Mom and Dad told me not to stress about the money part, but whenever someone told me the deposit amount they needed, I would freak out."

"We had a great wedding, babe," Eli tells her, slipping his arm around her shoulders. He presses his lips to her temple. "You did good."

I watch them, how easy they are with each other, though they went through some tough times to get to this place. Tougher than almost all of us, save Diego and Jocelyn. I used to hate Eli with everything I had. Sometimes I still get annoyed with him, not gonna lie, but he treats my sister like a queen and he's a good dad to my niece and nephew, so I can't complain.

The media eats up our rivalry though. We were even on the cover of one of the top sports magazines when the season kicked off, standing back-to-back, staring at the camera with serious expressions, our arms crossed in front of our chests.

Eli absolutely loves that type of shit. Me? I could take it or leave it.

"We're having a hard time finding a place to have the reception," Hannah says, her voice low. Almost like she doesn't want to admit she's having trouble. "We're using a wedding planner, and she's fabulous, but because our wedding date is only a few months away, pretty much everything is booked. We're on a couple of waitlists, but I don't know…"

"I told Hannah we should run away to Hawaii and have a destination wedding," I suggest.

Ava immediately says no—I swear the only reason she does is because her greatest joy in life is disagreeing with me.

Eli's expression turns thoughtful as he rubs his chin. "That's not a bad idea."

I sit up straighter, shock coursing through me. "You think so, huh?"

"For sure. I mean, I'm down for a party, no matter where it's at. Flashy wedding reception in Phoenix or on a tropical island. I'm down."

"We wouldn't invite nearly as many people if we had a destination wedding," Hannah points out. "We'd keep it small."

"Aw, that would be a shame," Ava says. "Have you looked into another location? Like, another city?"

"That seems like such a hassle," Hannah says. "It's hard enough trying to plan it here."

I silently agree with her.

"If you need help, just call me," Ava offers. "I love planning stuff."

"You have two small children to raise. You're kind of busy."

"Hey, Eli's mom is with us a lot now, taking care of the kids." Ava smiles up at her husband. "She's with them now. I can help with whatever you need. Or even when they're napping. My mother-in-law is a pretty terrific planner too. She would probably have some good ideas."

Eli's mom used to be a bit of a mess, but after that car accident and the DUI she got, she's come around. She's not drinking anymore, which is huge, and she's gotten a lot closer with Eli and Ava.

Hannah looks ready to cry at the offer of help, I swear to God. "I don't want to impose."

"Oh stop." Ava reaches across the table and grabs Hannah's hand. "We're family. That's what we do—help each other."

It's my turn to sling my arm around my woman's shoulders. I give Hannah a squeeze, because I can sense she's getting emotional. She's probably overwhelmed by Ava's support. "We're going to get through this."

Hannah turns her head, her gaze meeting mine. "I hate that you just said that. I know what you mean, but this is our wedding we're talking about. Instead of getting through this, as you said, we should be excited about our upcoming nuptials."

Leaning in close, I press my forehead to hers, my gaze never wavering. "This is why we should plan a destination wedding. Forget all these nerve-wracking wedding plans and waiting to see if we'll actually get a venue for our reception. You've got deposits on stuff and we don't even know if we have a place for the reception yet."

"I got the estimate for the flowers Friday," she whispers. "Fifty thousand dollars. And that's on the conservative side."

I pull away from her, blinking. Flowers that will die for fifty thousand dollars? I'm a guy. I'm the last person to think that makes sense, but I will go with whatever Hannah thinks is best. "That seems like...a lot."

"It is." She glances over at Ava and Eli, who are literally kissing at the table. Jesus. "Maybe the destination wedding thing wouldn't be so bad."

"You know who had a destination wedding?"

"Who?"

"My parents." How could I forget? "They ran away to Hawaii, just like I want to."

Hannah stares at me, and I can practically see her brain

working. She's considering the idea, and it's about damn time. "Maybe we should."

"We totally should."

She sinks her teeth into her lower lip, and I stare at her mouth. She has the best lips—plump and smooth. I like nibbling on them too. "We might lose money on some of the deposits."

"Fuck it. I don't really care. I'd rather run away with you. And our family and friends. We don't need to make a big splash and stress ourselves out over this wedding, Hannah. I just want to be with you." I cup her cheek, tilting her face up so her shining eyes meet mine. "I love you, and I don't need to prove that in front of six hundred people. Let's go to Hawaii. I'll call a travel agent and they can find a giant beach house for all of us to stay at."

"What are you two planning over there?"

At Ava's question, we both glance over at her and Eli, and I smile at my sister. "Trying to figure out this wedding bullshit."

Ava frowns. Eli laughs.

"Should you really call it *bullshit*?" Ava asks, her brows drawn together in concern. "This is your marriage you're talking about."

Eli covers up his chuckling with a cough, pressing his fist against his mouth.

"But it is bullshit," Hannah says calmly. "I'm over it."

"Me too."

Hannah cuts a glance in my direction. "I'm thinking Jake is right. We should plan a destination wedding."

Ava smiles. "Didn't Mom and Dad do the same thing?"

I nod. "Yeah. They did. I think they were on to something."

"You should do it," Eli says. "We could all stand to take a little vacation after the football season."

"Right?" I lean back in my chair, toying with the ends of Hannah's hair with my fingers. It's the longest it's ever been. I think mostly because she doesn't make time to get it cut. She tends to get forgetful when she's wrapped up in a project, which is most days. "After we beat you in the playoffs and go on to win the Super Bowl, I'll be ready for rest and relaxation. Oh, and a wedding."

Hannah flashes me a smile. Ava laughs.

Eli scowls.

"You wanna put money on that prediction?" he asks.

I lean forward. "We can't, Eli. It's illegal. Remember?"

Ava groans. "Why are we even having this conversation?"

Eli ignores his wife. "We don't have to call it a bet. Money won't be involved."

"What are you suggesting?" I raise my brows.

"This is a bad idea," Ava protests.

"You guys," Hannah adds.

We continue ignoring them.

"Whoever wins gets to have first pick at next year's Thanksgiving family football game." Eli thrusts his hand out toward me. "You down?"

Considering my dad always lets me have first pick at our annual football game on Thanksgiving, this is just Eli trying to one up me. Typical. "Deal." I shake his hand.

"This is silly." Ava shakes her head.

"At least make it interesting," Hannah says. "Like, whoever loses has to streak or skinny dip at the pool at whatever place we're staying in Hawaii."

"What if we both lose?" I ask her.

Her eyes twinkle devilishly. "Then you both have to streak."

"I'm game. I could give two shits who sees my junk."

Hannah rolls her eyes at Eli's statement. "I don't really want to see it."

"I don't want everyone seeing it either." This comes from Ava, making Eli laugh.

I nudge my shoulder against Hannah's. "Think that was a stupid bet?"

"Not at all." She shakes her head, her smile growing. "Pretty sure you've got this one in the bag."

CHAPTER 3

HANNAH

 *ive months later...*

"THE PRIVATE CAR IS HERE," I say after I receive a text from the driver. I send him a quick reply, letting him know we'll be right out. "Guess it's time to go."

Jake smiles at me from where he's sitting on the couch. "You excited?"

I nod. "I'll miss you."

He makes a dismissive noise. "No, you won't. You'll be with your friends, partying it up all weekend."

I laugh, not bothering to deny it. It's my bachelorette weekend and I know the plans that have been made will be completely over the top. Ava and Autumn put it all together, with a little help from their mom and my future mother-in-law, Fable.

I'm completely in the dark. I don't even know exactly where we're going. I was told to bring lots of warm weather clothes and a couple of sparkly, sexy dresses to go out in at night.

Considering I don't own too many sparkly, sexy dresses, I had to go shopping. For dresses, for shoes, for bikinis and makeup. I even had to purchase new luggage.

This past football season, I didn't travel much with Jake. I was too busy putting together my art show. Or planning our original wedding. Thank God that got cancelled.

Our destination wedding on Maui is happening in two weeks, and I'm not even stressed about it. We found an organizer on the island who took care of everything. We gave her a (huge) budget and Jake basically told her the sky was the limit, so she went for it.

Turns out our Hawaiian wedding will still be cheaper than the one we were originally planning. The best thing?

Everyone we know and love who we invited can make it.

We both can't wait.

"Let me help you." Jake gets off the couch and heads for the foyer, where my luggage is waiting. I grab the smaller suitcase, while he takes the big one, and we walk outside to where the driver is standing close to the back end of the sleek black SUV he's driving. He hits a button and the rear door rises before he's heading for us and taking my luggage, so he can put it into the back of the vehicle.

Jake turns to me and pulls me into his arms. "Have fun," he murmurs against my temple, his arms squeezing me tight. "I'm gonna miss you."

"I'll miss you too." I pull away slightly, so he can bend down and kiss me. "Love you."

"Don't do anything crazy," he murmurs against my lips, right before he gives me a soul-stealing kiss.

He would do something like that, right before I have to leave. Now my body is all tingly and my head is spinning, while he's grinning like he knows exactly what he did to me as he shoves me into the back seat of the car.

The SUV's engine is running, so I hit the button and the tinted window slides down. Jake is still standing there, his hands in his pockets and a big grin on his face.

"You look really cocky right now," I tease him.

His grin only intensifies. "You are looking at a Super Bowl champion, you know."

I roll my eyes, and he chuckles, shaking his head. I'm so incredibly proud of this man and all that he's accomplished in a short amount of time. From high school to college to the NFL, he has worked toward his goal with an intensity that some almost fear.

Not me. Never me. I know what this man is really like. Deep down, he's sweet and encouraging and supportive. He's smart and he's giving and he's loyal. He's also not a quitter.

And in a few short weeks, he's going to be my husband.

"I'm going to miss you," I whisper, hating the sudden clog in my throat. I rest my hand on the door handle, about to open it and climb out, so I don't have to leave after all.

I'd rather stay home with him.

Jake takes a step forward, his hands curling around the bottom window frame, his face practically in mine. "You'll be having too much fun with everyone to miss me, babe. You're going to see Sophie, remember? You've really been looking forward to that."

My smile is shaky, and I let it fade. "I don't leave you very often. You're the one who's always leaving me. I'm used to that. I'm not used to…this."

He leans his head into the car, his mouth finding mine. The kiss is firm and when he pulls away, his blue eyes are blazing into mine. "I love you. Come back to me."

Oh. That is so…romantic.

"Promise me." His voice is fierce, as is his expression.

"I promise," I murmur, making him smile.

The sight of that smile makes my heart flutter.

* * *

By the time I'm walking up the stairs and into the private plane, I'm an overemotional, excited wreck, but in the best way. Ava and Autumn are already waiting inside, since they flew into Phoenix on the private jet their parents arranged for our trip, while Jocelyn accompanied them, since she lives in Seattle like Ava. Gracie and Hayden just joined us too, having arrived on a flight from California.

I'm not particularly close to Gracie and Hayden, but when we were in college, I would come home those first couple of summers after classes ended and we'd all hang out. They're super sweet and fun and they accepted me into their friend group with open arms. They're both teachers—Hayden, at a private school in San Francisco, and Gracie, at the elementary school I attended.

Gracie also happens to be very, very pregnant.

"Are you sure it's okay for you to fly?" Ava asks her as we all watch Gracie settle into her seat.

More like she fell back into it. That belly of hers is pretty big, and she's a tall, extremely thin woman. She looks like she's carrying a basketball under the black T-shirt dress she's wearing.

"I'm fine." She rests her hand over her belly, running it up and down. "Caleb's mother recently told me he weighed almost ten pounds when he was born."

Ava and Autumn share a look, but otherwise say nothing.

In fact, all of us say nothing as we absorb that particular fact. Hayden breaks the silence first.

"Ten pounds? Really?"

Gracie nods.

"That child is going to split you in two if he weighs ten pounds." Hayden nods toward Gracie's protruding stomach, her eyes wide.

I'm sure I'm staring too, but I keep my mouth shut. I don't need to freak Gracie out any more than she probably already is.

"Shh. Don't say that," Autumn chastises, pasting on a serene smile for Gracie's benefit. "You'll be fine. It's amazing what our bodies can do during childbirth."

Gracie snorts. "If this baby is actually ten pounds, I'm having a C-section. No way am I letting a ten-pound monster come out my vag."

I can't help but grimace, and Hayden sends me the same look. We're the only ones who haven't been pregnant on this plane, and I'm okay with it. From what I can tell, Hayden is too.

"Too bad you don't get to drink on this trip," Ava says, sitting in the seat next to Gracie, already clutching a glass of champagne in her fingers. "I'm consuming as much alcohol as I can while I'm child-free."

"Same here. Thank God for our mothers," Autumn agrees, snatching up her own glass of champagne and clinking it against her sister's. "I'm praying ours doesn't call me before we take off and beg me to come back."

"She won't," Ava says assuredly. "If my mother-in-law can handle my tiny terrors, then Mom can handle yours."

Fable is watching Autumn and Ash's twins while Eli's mom is watching their kids for the weekend. The guys are all getting together at our place while we girls are away, and I'm sure they're going to be up to no good.

Jake told me he didn't think any strippers would be involved, but I don't know. I don't trust Diego and Caleb. Or Eli.

Strippers will probably be part of their bachelor weekend plans. And I'm okay with it. Seriously. I trust my man.

"Guys, I don't even know where we're going." I grab one of the last glasses of champagne the flight attendant poured for us and take a sip, the alcohol cool and crisp on my tongue. "Can you tell me yet? Or do I have to wait until we arrive?"

Everyone looks at each other before turning their attention on me.

"We're going to…." Ava hesitates before they all shout:

MIAMI!

"Wait, really? Miami?" I've never been there. We've been to Florida before—Orlando, on a trip to Disney World a long time ago—but not Miami, so I'm kind of excited.

Okay, I'm really excited.

"We rented a house and it's so gorgeous, Hannah. Really close to the beach and shopping and restaurants. It has a bazillion bedrooms and there's a pool. It's going to be sun, sand and hot Miami nights!" Autumn starts shimmying in her seat, raising the champagne glass above her head like she's dancing at a nightclub, and the rest of them join in.

I do too.

My mouth already hurts from smiling too much. My heart is so full, and I'm overwhelmed with gratitude. When I was in high school, I didn't have a lot of friends. I definitely wasn't a popular girl—not even close. I was quiet and kept to myself and I liked it that way.

All of these women have taken me in over the years and embraced me into their friend group; two of them are even going to be my sisters-in-law. As my gaze takes them all in while they're talking and laughing, I feel so incredibly lucky in this moment.

My family is small. Just my mom and her boyfriend, who I've grown to care about over the years, only because he takes such good care of my mother. My only sibling is my older brother, Joe. He's married and has a son, and they'll be at our wedding.

I can't wait to see all of them. I miss my mom. My brother and I have grown closer the last couple of years, ever since he got out of the Navy and is now living the civilian life. He's in California, back in our hometown, and Mom lives with him and his family, when she's not staying the night at her boyfriend's house.

It's reassuring, knowing that they have each other. She relied on me for so long after Joe made his escape, right out of high school. It's a huge help, for him to step in and be there for her.

Still miss them both though.

"Hey, Hannah. Can I talk to you for a moment?"

I turn to find Hayden standing in front of me, her expression somber.

"Sure. What is it?"

"Look, I know Sophie is going to be there. She's meeting us in Miami." Hayden pauses for a moment, and I notice the worry flickering in her gaze. "And I know she used to date Tony back in high school."

I smile as a flood of memories wash over me. It's been even longer since I saw Sophie. We drifted apart after she moved but have reconnected the last couple of years, which has been wonderful. I didn't realize how much I missed her until I had her back in my life. "Those were good times. We were the two quiet girls who nabbed the hot guys on the football team."

"Right. Tony told me. Well, he didn't say he was a hot guy or that Sophie nabbed him, but he did tell me they were together."

"They won homecoming king and queen that year," I say, remembering how badly I wanted to win with Jake.

And how equally happy I was that my best friend won instead.

"Yeah. They were like, the perfect high school couple." Hayden sighs, the sound full of sadness.

Which is startling because Hayden is one of the most confident people I know.

"No, they really weren't," I say.

Her gaze meets mine. "They weren't?"

I shake my head. "Back then, Sophie wasn't the greatest at communication. Neither was Tony. She was pushing him away because a lot of other stuff was going on in her life. Next thing we knew, she was accepted to a dance school, and she moved away. Tony was heartbroken."

"Right, because he loved her so much."

"Maybe they were in love, but that was a long time ago, and it was more like first love stuff, you know? They were only together for a couple of months." I smile at her. "You and Tony have been together a lot longer."

Hayden smiles faintly. "I just—I don't want Sophie to hate me."

I frown. "Why would she hate you?"

"Because I'm married to her first boyfriend. And you're her best friend. She might think I'm trying to tread on her territory or whatever," Hayden explains.

I stare at her, noting the nervousness in her gaze. How agitated she seems. Like she can't stop fidgeting. "Sophie definitely won't hate you. She's living her best life, traveling the world with her dance troupe."

She studied in London for years and now performs with a world-renowned dance company. I was surprised she's able to make it to both my bachelorette weekend and wedding, but this is the time of year when they take a break, so that worked out.

"Are you sure? I want us all to get along. I don't want any

friction this weekend. This is your time to have fun. We're celebrating you. I don't want any hard feelings between any of us." Hayden's smile is tentative, and I can't help it.

I pull her in for a hug.

"It's going to be great," I murmur, breathing in her rich girl scent. Her dad is loaded, as is Tony's, and everything Hayden does and wears and says just screams money to me. "You and Sophie are going to love each other. She can tell you funny stories about Tony, and you can do the same."

Hayden pulls away, smiling at me. "Thank you for inviting me. I know we're not that close, though Jake and Tony are. Jake is one of Tony's best friends."

"I swear, they all try to claim Tony as a best friend. Even Eli," Ava adds to our conversation.

I just smile. Ava is an eavesdropper sometimes, but I don't mind. It's in her blood. Jake says she's done it since he can remember.

"Ladies, we're going to be taking off here in a few minutes for our trip to Miami, so please find your seats and prepare for takeoff," says the pilot over the intercom.

I drain my glass of champagne and hand it to the flight attendant, who's been taking care of us since we walked onto the plane, then go find a seat.

This weekend, surrounded by women I love and adore, is going to be amazing.

CHAPTER 4

HANNAH

"Oh. My. God!" I squeal the moment I set eyes on Sophie, who's standing in the middle of the sleek, modern kitchen of the equally sleek, modern house my friends booked for my bachelorette weekend celebration.

My childhood best friend smiles and throws her arms out as I run to her, embracing her so hard, I almost knock her over. Breathless laughter escapes her as she squeezes her arms around me. She's so thin, yet lean. All muscle, thanks to years and years of dancing.

"It's been so long," I tell her when I finally pull away. I can hear the distant chatter of my other friends as they wander around the house, and it feels good that they're leaving us alone for a bit.

"Too long," Sophie says, nudging her shoulder against mine. "I can't believe you're getting married."

"I know." Sometimes, I can't believe it either.

"To *Jake Callahan*," she adds, giving me major nostalgic vibes. I feel like we're back at school, gossiping about the cool kids, which we were definitely not a part of. "He was the most popular boy in our class. Now he's a freaking NFL superstar."

"Pinch me." I hold my arm out to her. "I must be dreaming."

Sophie pinches me—hard, I might add—making me yelp. Then we start laughing all over again. This is how the rest of the women find us when they enter the kitchen a few minutes later. The two of us trying to talk over each other and collapsing into a fit of giggles every time we bring up some old, funny memory.

"Sophie!" Ava goes to her and wraps her up in a big hug. "It's so good to see you! I've been keeping up on your career. My daughter is taking ballet."

"So is mine," Jocelyn says, nudging Ava out of the way so she can hug Sophie too. "We're so proud of you. Every time I see yet another beautiful photo of you dancing on social media, I think, 'I know her!'"

Sophie and I share a look. The once unattainable popular crowd from high school is now embracing her fully, and it's kind of funny. I've grown used to the feeling of their acceptance. Once Jake and I started dating, I was pulled into the group because of him. At first, it was awkward, because a lot of those boys didn't like me much—specifically Diego. He viewed me as an outsider, trying to steal away his best friend.

Then he went through his own bullshit with Jocelyn and forgot all about me dating his best friend.

We catch up for a few minutes, all of us standing around the pristine white marble counter, throwing all sorts of questions at Sophie as she tries her best to answer them all. The only one who remains quiet is Hayden, who I can tell is watching Sophie carefully. Probably trying to figure her out.

I guess I can't blame her. If I was going to spend the entire weekend with my husband's high school girlfriend, I think I'd be giving her the once over too.

Speaking of...

"Whatever happened to Cami Lockhart?" I ask out of the blue. "Anyone know?"

The women go silent for what feels like a lifetime—probably only about thirty seconds—before Jocelyn answers.

"Last I heard, she married some older CEO-type and is living her best life as his trophy wife." Jocelyn scowls. "I shouldn't say this, but I still hate her."

"Same," Ava murmurs as I nod my head in agreement.

The three of us had to deal with Cami in high school, in not so pleasant ways. And that's putting it mildly. I'm not even touching on the bullshit Cami did.

She was the worst.

"You have reason to hate her the most out of all of us," I tell Jocelyn, slipping my arm around her shoulders and pulling her into my side. She smiles at me, resting her head on my shoulder for a brief moment before she pulls away.

"We are not going to sit around and talk about shitty people. This is your weekend, Hannah. We're celebrating you!" Jocelyn glances around at everyone else, encouraging them to shout their agreement. "Let's go upstairs and show you your room."

"I can share with someone if I have to," I say, as they practically drag me up the stairs, my gaze eating up the décor as I walk past it.

I have seen my fair share of expensive homes. Being with Jake has opened up my eyes to a whole different world.

This house is right up there as one of the most beautiful I've ever seen.

"How much did this place cost?" I ask, as I stare at the artwork lining the upstairs hallway's walls. "And why is it on Airbnb?"

"It's not," Autumn calls as she leads the way to my room. There are multiple bedrooms upstairs, every one of them light and airy and spacious, with giant windows and amazing views. "One of the players' wives told me about this website where you can book high-end homes that you can't find anywhere else."

Autumn's husband plays for the NFL too. It's kind of wild, how many of the guys from our community play professionally. We all came from humble beginnings.

Well, not the Callahans. Jake's father comes from wealth. His mom, though? I think she might've been poorer than me growing up.

Fable told me a long time ago history repeats itself generationally. Most of the time, it's good, and sometimes, it's bad. She feels like both me and Jake, and Autumn and Ash are similar to how her and Drew were when they were younger.

"Here you go!" Autumn pushes the main bedroom's door open wider, and they all step back to let me enter first.

"Oh wow." I go straight to the window, staring out at the shimmering blue water. The equally bright blue sky above, dotted with the occasional fluffy white cloud. Glancing down, I see the infinity pool and all the empty loungers surrounding it, and I turn from the window to smile at my friends.

"Who are we still waiting on?"

"Ellie," Ava answers. "Her plane should be landing in an hour or so."

"Shall we wait for her out by the pool?"

"Definitely," Hayden says, sharing a look with Gracie. "Let's go put on our swimsuits and meet down there."

As everyone starts to leave the room, I call Sophie's name, wanting her to stay behind with me.

"Want to share my room?" I ask her once they're all gone.

Sophie tilts her head, studying me. Her hair is long and still so blonde, and she's got it up in a high ponytail that swings with her every step. "Are you sure you don't want

29

the room to yourself? I'm sure I can share with someone else."

I mentally count who's here this weekend and realize that Sophie would be the odd woman out if I *don't* share with her. "I want you to share my room. We can stay up too late gossiping, like we used to."

Sophie's eyes actually start to fill with tears, and she embraces me again, clinging to me, her face pressed against my shoulder. I swear I feel her tears soak into my shirt and I can't help it.

I start crying too.

"I'm so happy for you," Sophie says as she pulls away. "You have everything you could ever want. A man who loves you. A great career. Hannah Walsh, you are living your absolute best life."

"I know, right?" I begin to cry harder. "Sometimes… sometimes I worry it might all disappear, you know? Like I'll wake up one morning, and it will all have been a dream."

"No." Sophie shakes her head, wiping the tears from her cheeks. "Nope. You're not dreaming. It's all happening."

I frown. "Didn't some chick from one of our favorite reality shows have a tattoo that said that? 'It's all happening'?"

Sophie bursts out laughing, shaking her head. "Only you would remember that."

"I'm right, though, aren't I? That one chick who thought she could sing and got married wearing a crop top wedding gown."

"Please. *Please* tell me you're wearing a crop top wedding gown." Sophie is doing this weird laughing-crying thing that's kind of hilarious.

"I am getting married on a tropical island, so maybe I should."

Sophie sobers right up. "I'm kidding. You know that, right?"

I roll my eyes. "I am too, ya goof."

We smile at each other.

"I need to go get my suitcase and bring it up here," Sophie says.

"We have a butler for the weekend. He can bring it up for you, Sophie."

We turn to find Autumn standing in the doorway, already clad in a black bikini and a sheer, flowing tropical print coverup.

"A butler?" I raise my brows.

Autumn nods, beaming. "We pulled out all the stops for your weekend, Hannah. Once Ellie shows up, the celebration can really begin! I'll let the butler know to bring up your suitcase, Soph. And then you two need to hurry up and change and come hang out at the pool!"

She's gone before we can say another word.

"A butler?" I ask again, turning to Sophie.

"A butler, and a personal chef. Housekeepers. I heard there will even be a bartender making a custom drink for us in honor of you," Sophie says.

"I can't believe this." They really went overboard for me. It's kind of mind-blowing.

"Believe it, babe." Sophie smiles. "This weekend is all for you, so enjoy it."

CHAPTER 5

HAYDEN

*W*e've been lounging by the pool all afternoon, soaking up the sun and munching on snacks. The alcohol is flowing, and my best friend is grumpy because she can't drink a drop.

"I don't even drink that much and I'm dying to get wasted." Gracie crosses her arms over her bare belly—yes, she's wearing a white bikini, which looks amazing against her olive skin—and pouts.

"I bet the bartender can make you a virgin piña colada." I nod toward the very attractive, shirtless bartender, who's currently got a blender going as he makes another batch of non-virginal piña coladas for a few of us ladies.

Ellie arrived a couple of hours ago and she's full of stories of life on the road with her rock star boyfriend Jackson. We're all sitting in a row on the loungers, the thick cushion comfortable and soft. The warm sun and the gentle breeze lull me into drowsiness and it's difficult for me to keep my eyes open for an extended period of time.

Thank God for the sunglasses I'm wearing. No one can tell I'm falling asleep.

"Are you falling asleep?" Gracie asks minutes later, slapping my arm.

I startle, turning my head to glare at her. "What's wrong with you?"

She squirms around on the lounger as if she can't get comfortable. "I want this thing out of me."

"What thing? Wait, are you referring to your unborn child as a *thing*?" I lower my sunglasses, so she can see the shock in my gaze.

Gracie rolls her eyes, not impressed. "This thing. This monster. This giant man-baby that won't stop growing. Whatever you want to call him. I want him out."

"How far along are you again?" I can't keep track with the weeks or months. All I know is, Gracie appears big enough to pop.

"I'm far along enough to birth him and be done with it." Her eyes grow wide and she drops her arms at her side, staring up at the sky. I don't know how she's doing it, considering she's looking right into the sun. "It's so weird. When you're first pregnant, you're so excited and scared and nervous. Then you start to grow and show, and you freak out. No way am I birthing a baby. This little sucker is staying inside of me forever, thank you very much."

I grimace but keep my thoughts to myself.

"Then you get to the point where I am and you're like, get it out of me noooooowwwwww." She drags the word on forever, and she's loud enough that she's gaining attention.

"Girl, I feel you. I was you," Ava shouts from her spot a few loungers over.

"None of you can complain. I carried twins," Autumn adds.

"Yeah, but you had a C-section. I at least birthed both my babies naturally."

Only the Callahan sisters would turn childbirth into a competition, I swear to God.

"I was a teen mom."

That's all Jocelyn has to say. She wins.

"You're really quiet," Gracie observes.

I shrug. "I have nothing to add to this birthing conversation." Thank God.

I'll have babies later. I'm thinking early thirties? There is no rush to have a child. Though I would love to see a black-haired, dark-eyed handsome little baby boy who looks just like his dad in my arms…

"Are you okay?" Gracie's question pulls me right out of my baby dreaming.

Ugh. Hanging around these women is already affecting me in a weird way.

"I'm fine." A sigh leaves me and I sneak yet another glance at Sophie. God, she's beautiful. Tall and toned, her arms and legs defined with muscle. Her stomach flat as can be. She moves with an elegant grace that comes naturally from the many years of dance training.

It's weird, knowing that once upon a time, she was Tony's girlfriend. That they were together in high school. That she kissed him and won homecoming with him, and that they share so many special memories.

Tony and I share a lot of special memories too, but that woman intimidates the crap out of me.

And not many people intimidate me.

"Is it Sophie?" At her question, I jerk my head in Gracie's direction. Her voice is low, and no one is paying attention to us. "I bet it's kind of weird, having her here."

Another sigh leaves me and I decide to be truthful with my friend. I already told Hannah how I felt about Sophie joining us for the weekend. I'm cool with it. She's one of

Hannah's oldest, dearest friends. I thought I could handle it because, in the end, I'm the one with Tony, right? Lucky me.

And I am lucky. I know I am. Tony is a great husband. I love and adore him, and I know he feels the same about me.

It's weirder than I thought it would be though, having the gorgeous, popular ballet dancer in our midst. She's been in *Vogue* magazine, for God's sake. *Vogue!* When I was in my early teens, that was my biggest dream. I thought I could be a model and travel the world, wearing the most popular fashions.

Ha. In my dreams.

Yet this woman is living my dream. At one point, I thought I could be a dancer too. Though I suppose a lot of us thought that when we were younger. When our dreams felt attainable and our potential endless.

Reality has a way of crashing down on us, reminding us that we do have limits. Sometimes, we can't make all of our dreams come true.

"She's gorgeous. Successful. She travels the world and has done so much in such a short amount of time." My voice is wistful, and I see the scowl form on my best friend's face.

"Please. Have you seen her feet? They're hideous."

I can't help but laugh. Leave it to Gracie to defend me and find the one flaw on the otherwise perfect Sophie. "Gracie."

"What? It's true! Being a dancer is tough on your feet! I caught a glimpse of them earlier and yikes." Gracie mock shivers. "You can see them right now if you lean forward a little."

I don't lean forward. I don't need to see Sophie's feet. I already have, and damn it, Gracie is right.

They're kind of hideous.

But they're her work instrument. Of course, they're beat-up and calloused, and her toes are a little knotty looking.

She's on them all day long, twirling and spinning and jumping and whatever else it is that famous ballerinas do.

"Don't be mean," I chastise her.

"I'm just speaking truths. Being pregnant makes me too honest, I guess."

"More like being pregnant makes you grouchy," I toss back at her.

She grabs the lemon from her glass of melting ice water and tosses it at me. It lands on my arm, the cold fruit making me squeal when it hits my warm skin. I pick it up and fling it back at her, and it lands dead center on her protruding belly.

"What are you two doing down there?" Jocelyn calls. "Fighting?"

"Do we need to separate you?" Ellie asks. "You're as bad as Autumn and Ava."

"She's grumpy." I point at Gracie. "Pregnancy makes her mad."

"Caleb makes me mad," Gracie adds. "He did this to me."

"Oh please! You were willing!" Ava shouts.

"Wonder how the guys are," Gracie says to me once everyone stops yelling at us.

They were getting together in Phoenix for the weekend to have an extended bachelor party.

"Caleb said he hired strippers," Gracie continues before I can say anything. "I told him if he gets a lap dance, I will kill him."

"He won't get a lap dance. This is all for Jake." I chance a glance in Hannah's direction. "Though his future wife will probably kill him if he gets a lap dance."

"I don't care about strippers," Hannah says, completely nonchalant. "Just—no touching allowed."

"What if I told you we hired male strippers for this weekend?"

Gracie sits up straighter, her eyes wide. "You did not."

"You're right." I shrug. "I didn't."

But Ava and Autumn did.

Eventually, I head inside the house to use the bathroom and get out of the sun for a few minutes. I take my time meandering through the house, finding a small bathroom close to the front door. I sniff the soaps and run my hands over the extra soft towels, and when I'm finally starting for the back yard, I come across Sophie in the kitchen.

Alone.

"Oh." She waves the banana in her hand at me. "Hi."

"Hey." I stop on the other side of the counter across from her. "It's so great to finally meet you."

"Yeah. Same here." She takes me in for a moment, blatantly staring at me. I do the same to her. "It's kind of weird."

"Right? It's so weird."

"He has a type." She points at her hair. "He likes blondes."

"True." I decide to say what's been on my mind from the moment I knew she was coming. "You don't hate me, do you?"

Sophie frowns. "Why would I hate you?"

"Because I'm married to your high school boyfriend." The moment the words leave me, I realize how dumb they sound.

"I don't even know you, but I hear good things about you. Hannah adores you. She says you're good for Tony. You bring him out of his quiet shell." Sophie's gaze grows distant. As if she's lost in her memories. "We were too quiet together. Maybe that was our problem. Plus, I was so young, and I didn't know how to express my feelings right. Then I moved and it was over."

Tony has told me a very summarized and similar version of that ending story. "Can I admit something?"

"Sure."

"I'm glad you moved. I'm glad I met Tony less than a year

later, and that we're still together now." I smile just thinking of him. "I hate to say it like that. I sound bitchy."

"No, you sound honest, and there's nothing wrong with that. My loss is your gain. You two sound perfect for each other, and I mean that in the nicest way." She smiles. "It feels good, being here this weekend. Seeing Hannah so happy, surrounded by her friends. You've all been so good to her, and I sort of abandoned her and Tony our senior year."

"Are you happy?" When she starts to say something, I interrupt her, unable to help myself. "I mean, truly happy? Your life looks fantastic. You're living the dream."

A fond smile curls her lips. "I'm happy. My dream is a lot of hard work and it's demanding, I can't lie. But I love it. I love my life right now. I'm seeing someone. He's a dancer too, and he understands the lifestyle. How grueling it is. This isn't for the faint of heart."

"I'm sure it's not." It's a relief to hear she has someone. I don't want her pining away for her lost love and hating me for being with him. "Thank you for being honest with me."

"I think we could be friends," Sophie says.

I smile at her. "I think we could be too."

CHAPTER 6

ASH

*W*e're at a hotel bar in Phoenix, but this isn't some cheesy place where there's a band playing eighties classics while the slick bartender flirts with all the single ladies.

Every Callahan I know has taste, and it's easy to have it when you also have money.

And the Callahans have a lot of that too.

Lucky me, I married one. Though I didn't marry Autumn for her money, that's for sure. When I first met her, that part of her life turned me off. Filled me with disgust. Of course, I was a broke-ass joke, with a giant chip on my shoulder, who trusted no one. My life had been filled with one disappointment after another until eventually, I did my best to turn off my emotions and just skate through life.

Until I started spending more time with Autumn. That girl...

Damn. She rocked my world. She still does. Even now, when she's exhausted after chasing after our twins, day in and day out, and she collapses in bed at nine, falling asleep the moment her head hits the pillow.

I stare at her in wonder sometimes when she's sleeping like that. Her lips pursed and her dark hair in complete disarray. I touch her face, flooded with memories of our life together. What we've created. I even think about what's to come. What more can we create?

A lot.

Happiness is watching the mother of my children laugh as she teases them. Chases after them through the house, their little feet taking them as fast as they can go. I always join in on the action, snagging one of them up and tossing them into the air, their giggles and squeals making my heart expand to the point I don't think I'll be able to keep it in my chest.

How'd I get so lucky?

Life threw me a bunch of shit, namely my mother. Once I got her out of my life and was firmly embraced by the Callahan family, I never looked back. It sounds corny even in my own head, but they nurtured me. Taught me how to take care of myself, to stand up for myself, to think for myself. All things my mother never bothered to help me learn.

"You're quiet."

I glance up at my brother-in-law's observation. I lift my glass in Eli's direction, then take a swig. "Nothing you're used to."

Eli grins. This motherfucker never shuts up. "Life is meant to be lived loudly."

"You got that written on a wooden sign hanging up on your laundry room wall?" This comes from Caleb. I'm the oldest of all of these fools, but at one point during high school, I either played with them or against them—Eli—and luckily, I enjoy hanging out with them.

Good thing, too, because it feels like I'm related to half of them through marriage, though really the number is only two. The rest of them just come along with Jake and Eli because they're all such good friends.

I may sound like I'm grumbling, but I'm not. There's nothing better than hanging out with this group of guys, and we don't do it as much as we used to. We're all so damn busy and scattered all over the country, it's difficult to make our schedules work to spend time together all at once.

A wedding will do that for you, though. Not only are we hanging out for the bachelor's weekend for Jake, but in three weeks, we'll all be together again on Maui, celebrating their actual wedding.

"I'm not as loud as you, Bennett." I lean forward, resting my forearms on the table. The bar we're in is dark and elegant, with subtle lighting and low music playing in the background. Not really the place for the obnoxious Eli Bennett to put on his usual show. "I'll let you have all the glory."

"Jake is the one who deserves all the glory," Tony says. He's my favorite of Jake's friends. He's quiet and thoughtful, and when he opens his mouth, he's always saying something I want to hear. "It's his weekend."

"And he won the Super Bowl," Jackson points out. "Can't forget that."

Eli grunts. "He won't let us *ever* forget it."

Jake smiles before taking a sip from his drink, making an ahhhh sound after he swallows. "Life is good, my friends."

"You still gonna hold me to the bet?" Eli asks.

We all perk up at that question.

"What bet?" I ask.

"It wasn't a bet." Jake scowls. "It's illegal, remember?"

"Please tell me he owes you a million bucks." This comes from Caleb.

"We need details," Jackson says.

Diego chuckles and shakes his head. I'm sure he knows all the details, since he plays on the same team with Eli.

"We came to an—agreement a few months ago. If one of us wins the Super Bowl, the other has to pay up." Jake smiles, looking pleased, though he doesn't say anything else.

"How? You're really telling us no money was involved?" Caleb grumbles. He likes to give us all shit for being rich while he's not, but he's not actually complaining. That guy is happier than a pig in shit, living in his cute house not too far from the lake, selling real estate while his hot wife Gracie is a teacher. They're happy as hell and she's getting ready to pop with their first kid.

"Don't forget to mention the best part," Diego says.

"What's the best part?" I ask.

Jake smirks. "Loser has to streak in Maui. Jump in the pool naked."

Eli shakes his head. "I ain't scared."

No. I don't imagine he is.

"You might scare all the children," Jackson says, laughing.

"And the mothers. Don't forget them." Diego laughs louder.

"You guys are idiots." Tony shakes his head, his expression full of contempt. "What the hell is wrong with you?"

"I didn't come up with the naked part. That was all Eli," Jake says, putting on an innocent face.

"You took the bait. You're just as bad as he is." Tony's gaze finds mine. "Don't you agree?"

See, Tony feels the same about me as I do about him. We're two kindred spirits in the chaos that is this friend group.

Grabbing my glass, I lift it in his direction. "Totally."

"Let's quit talking about my upcoming moment of humiliation and head back to the suite," Eli suggests, rubbing his hands together. "I have plans."

"What sort of plans?" Jake sounds wary, and he should be. I know what the plans are.

Strippers. Of course. Fucking Eli.

Though Caleb, Jackson and Diego are all guilty of putting this together. We have a group chat where all the bachelor weekend plans were made, and Eli mentioned strippers almost immediately. I said it might not be a good idea, but he ignored me.

Of course, he did.

Caleb encouraged it. As did Jackson and Diego. Tony was the only one who agreed with me, but it feels like the more we protested, the more they wanted it.

I quit complaining. So did Tony.

"Don't think too hard. You'll come up with the plans on your own," Tony says.

A weary exhale leaves our groom-to-be. "Strippers? Really?"

"Of course, we got strippers. You gotta live it up, bro. Soon you'll be tied down to your wifey and dream of the old days," Caleb says.

"Is that what you're doing? Dreaming of the old days every time you take a look at your pregnant wife?" Jake asks.

Caleb frowns. "No."

"We've all been with our women for a long-ass time," I point out. "You're the only one who had the giant horn-dog stage."

Jackson clears his throat. "Um, I went on tour a single man the summer after my first year of college."

They all start applauding and cheering him on.

Even me.

I had a small horn-dog stage, but I have no regrets getting with Autumn so young. When you know, you know. And I knew that girl was for me, even back then.

We eventually make our way back to the suite we got for

the weekend. Tomorrow, we play golf. The hotel resort we're staying at has an excellent course, and while the majority of us don't play that great, it's always fun, and we don't judge each other's golf game.

Well, there is a lot of shit-talking and whatnot, but that's expected. We're used to it.

A few minutes after our arrival at the suite, my phone dings with a text.

Wife: **What are you doing?**

Me: **Hanging out with strippers. You?**

She immediately FaceTimes me and I go out onto the patio to take her call.

"Are you serious? Let me see them." She's craning her neck, trying to look beyond me.

"I was kidding. There are no strippers." I pause. "Yet."

"Asher." Ooh, she busted out the full name. I know I'm in trouble. "Strippers? Really? Hannah is going to be pissed."

"Really, babe? I heard you guys will have strippers too."

Autumn's green eyes go wide. She is such a combination of her mom and dad, where Jake looks just like Drew. It's kind of wild, all the clones that have been created and that we're continuing to create. "No way."

"Don't play innocent with me. I don't care if you stuff a dollar bill down some asshole's G-string."

"Oh really? Because I have a problem if you stuff a dollar down some babe's G-string." Autumn's tone is haughty with a hint of pissed-off.

"I'm not interested in anyone else. Just you," I reassure her.

She's gone through some insecure stages after having the babies. They took a toll on her body and her mind, and she's been working hard to get back into shape. I have no complaints. There might be a bit more of her to love, but she's got those curves in all the right places. She hates her stretch marks, but to me, they're badges of honor after carrying not just one, but two babies.

I want more babies too, but if I even hint at it, she rolls her eyes and basically tells me to go fuck myself. Which I suppose I can't blame her. They're a handful, our children.

A lovable, rambunctious, over-the-top handful.

"Same," she murmurs, her eyes glowing as she stares at me. "I miss you."

"I miss you too."

"I wish you were here with me. You should see this house. It's gorgeous."

"We're staying in a pretty swanky place too." I flip my camera and show her the patio, before walking close to the giant floor-to-ceiling windows and giving her a view of inside. Some of the guys notice what I'm doing and they start waving. Caleb and Eli make vaguely obscene gestures.

I flip the camera back to me.

"Just another day with the guys?" she asks.

"You know it," I agree. "You're all having fun? Everyone's arrived?"

"We lounged at the pool all afternoon and now we're getting ready for a late dinner." Autumn lowers her voice. "Hayden and Sophie are really getting along. Almost like they're long-lost best friends or something."

"That's kind of weird."

"It actually makes sense, if you think about it. They're similar, meaning Tony goes for a certain type of woman. They share similar features too. They're both blonde."

"I've never been into blondes," I drawl as I settle into one of the overstuffed chairs.

"Good thing, considering." She flips her long, wavy dark hair over her shoulder, looking sassy. "Have fun, but not too much fun."

"Right back at you, babe." I smile, drinking her in. She

looks good. As pretty as I've ever seen her. She has a one-shouldered black sparkly dress on and her skin even shimmers, like she put on some sort of lotion with glitter in it.

Fuck, I miss her. I wish she were with me right now so I could drag her back to the bedroom and have my way with her.

"I love you," she murmurs.

"Love you too. You're beautiful."

Her smile is knowing. "I dressed up."

"You need to do that for me sometime." My tone is low.

Suggestive.

Her brows shoot up. "How about in Hawaii, when my mom is taking care of the kids for us, so we can go out? I can dress up for you then."

"Deal," I murmur.

"Bye. Oh, and don't forget!"

"Don't forget what?"

"You're not allowed to touch the strippers." She blows me a kiss and ends the call.

CHAPTER 7

HANNAH

*O*ur first night in Miami, we went out and practically shut the bars down in South Beach. I drank way too much.

So, so much.

But it was fun, cutting loose with my friends. Gracie was the only sober one there, and she ended up going back to the house early, since she was exhausted, and Ellie went back with her since she had jet lag.

Rough life, touring the world with your rock star boyfriend. Husband.

Wait. I don't think they're married yet.

I lounged in bed until almost noon and finally grabbed something to eat—thank you, personal chef hired just for the weekend—and we've spent the afternoon hanging out by the pool. The weather is fabulous. The food, amazing. The company?

Even better.

"I miss my kids," Ava declares after about two hours of continuous sunbathing. She has a big floppy hat on and a giant pair of sunglasses cover her eyes.

"I miss mine too," Autumn says, her lips barely moving. She's got her face tipped to the sun, her eyes also shielded by glasses, and she's wearing the tiniest olive-green bikini I've ever seen.

And this woman birthed twins.

"But not enough to want to rush back to them," Autumn continues, making everyone laugh. "I'm enjoying my weekend away, thank you, Hannah."

"I didn't plan this," I remind her. "You did."

Autumn lifts her glasses, so our gazes meet. "Thank you for getting married to our brother and giving us the excuse to celebrate."

"I heard they had strippers last night," Gracie calls out.

Tension immediately fills the air, and I can feel everyone looking at me, but they don't say anything.

"What?" I ask after approximately thirty seconds of silence. "Do you guys have a problem with them having strippers during Jake's bachelor party?"

"Yes," Gracie says indignantly.

"You're pregnant and irrational," Ava says. "Your opinion might throw the curve when the rest of us don't mind as much."

"I don't care. Women are throwing themselves at Jackson on a daily basis. I'm the one who's in his bed at night." Ellie smirks.

Ava tosses a pillow at her head.

"'My boyfriend is a hot rock star who writes songs about my vagina.'" Gracie rolls her eyes. "You're not allowed to have an opinion either."

"I really don't care about the strippers."

We all turn to look at Jocelyn, who has a bored expression on her face. I find this interesting, considering everyone thought at one point her man was cheating on her. And he sort of was, but not really?

It's hard to explain.

Plus, that was back in high school, which was a long time ago.

"You're really okay with it?" This comes from Sophie, who has zero skin in this game.

Jocelyn shrugs. "We've been together for so long, parents for so long, I actually encourage the guy to get out there and live a little. If he wants to watch some hot woman dance around for him and his friends, what's the harm in it? It's all in good fun."

"Ugh, you're so logical." Gracie runs her hand over her belly and sighs. "Caleb and I have had so much sex since I got pregnant, I really shouldn't worry about it. He's so into me."

"Tony was probably bored watching the strippers," Hayden says, her gaze going to Sophie's before they both start laughing.

Those two have become really good friends in a short amount of time. I guess it makes sense. It's nice to see them getting to know each other. They have a lot in common.

Like similar taste in men.

My phone rings with a FaceTime call and I realize it's my fiancé.

I answer immediately.

"Say hi to Jake, ladies!" I flip the camera so he can see everyone as they call hello and wave. Once they've settled down, I flip the camera back so he can see me.

His eyes are wide as he takes me in. "What are you wearing?"

I glance down at myself, remembering that I've got on a bright blue bikini that's not covering much. I don't wear swimsuits like this—it was a gift from my future sisters-in-law.

"You like it?" I pull the phone away so he can see more of me. "Your sisters gave it to me."

49

He whistles. Actually whistles.

"Tell them thank you." He's rubbing his jaw, contemplating me. "You need to bring that suit to Maui."

I laugh, his reaction making me forget all about the strippers. "Are you having a good time?"

"We were all hungover this morning. Thank God our tee time isn't until noon. We're headed to the golf course soon."

"Have fun." I wait a moment, fully expecting him to tell me about last night, but he just stares. Like he swallowed his tongue. "We went out to South Beach last night."

"How was it?"

"Packed. Hot. Fun." I brush a few stray hairs away from my face. "I drank too much."

"That's the point."

"What did you do last night?"

He rubs his jaw again, exhaling loudly. "You really want to know?"

I laugh. "I definitely want to know."

Glancing up, I find everyone watching me—or more like listening to Jake.

"Fine. Eli and Caleb hired a couple of strippers to show up to our suite."

"I knew it," Gracie whisper-hisses, Hayden shushing her.

"And how were they?"

"Eh." He shrugs one shoulder. "All right."

"Jacob Callahan, you need to tell us right now if anyone touched a stripper last night or got a lap dance." Ava appears out of nowhere behind me, no doubt looking ridiculous to her brother in the oversized shades and giant hat.

"Who the hell is that? Sounds like Ava."

"It is me, dipshit." She nudges me to the side and settles next to me, thrusting her face in close to my phone screen. I'm trying my best not to laugh. I know it'll only make her madder. "Did Eli get a lap dance?"

"No, Jesus. Chill out. He wouldn't do that."

"Did anyone get a lap dance?"

"I mean, some of us might've got grinded on."

"Like the groom-to-be?" I lift my brows.

Another ragged exhale leaves Jake, his expression pained. "Maybe?"

"Ooh, you're in trouble." Ava gets up and heads back to her lounger, satisfied with Jake's answer.

"Are you mad?" Jake's voice is low, his gaze full of worry.

Slowly, I shake my head. "No. Of course not. Isn't that the whole point of a bachelor weekend with your friends? Drinking and debauchery?"

"I didn't touch her. Not really. Not inappropriately."

"It's okay." I smile at him. "Just—don't complain when I tell you my stripper story tomorrow."

"You're going to have strippers too?" His dark brows draw together, his expression suddenly thunderous.

Uh oh.

"Rumor has it that it might happen."

"I don't like that."

"Tough shit, Jakey!" This comes from his older sister, of course. "It's too late! Some hot dudes are definitely showing up here tonight!"

"Hannah—"

"I trust you, you trust me, right?" I interrupt him.

He's only getting riled up thanks to his sisters. They know just how to push all of his buttons. They have a lifetime of experience under their belts.

"Of course, I trust you," he says.

"Then know I'm not going to do anything with some gross stripper." I have no idea if the strippers are going to be gross. Knowing Autumn and Ava, they probably hired some really good-looking guys.

I hope they did.

"I didn't think you would." He rolls his eyes. "My sisters drive me apeshit sometimes, I swear."

"We love you too, Jake!" Ava yells.

"I should've never FaceTimed you."

"I'm glad you did," I say, my voice soft. "This way, I get to look at you."

His expression eases, and I can see the tension leave him. He's come a long way from the angry teenager I first fell in love with. "I miss you."

"I miss you too." I smile, hating how tremulous my voice sounds. "I love you."

My friends start making kissy noises in the background and crooning words of mushy love, drowning out Jake's declaration that he loves me too.

But I read his lips. I know he said it—and that's good enough for me.

CHAPTER 8

JOCELYN

I haven't let loose like this since...
I don't know when.

When you become a mom at barely eighteen years old, your entire life changes. You're a grown-up, with grown-up responsibilities, whether you like it or not. I had a baby girl to take care of, and at the time of her birth, Diego and I weren't that close. I was still mad at him. I didn't trust him. We'd both just graduated high school, and my future felt uncertain.

It was a lot to deal with.

We've made it through some rough times, and now we have two beautiful children and a life I never thought could be real. My husband is a professional athlete, and he loves his job. He's really good at it too. He makes me proud. So do our children. Gigi is getting older and she's so dang smart. Sassy. Helpful. Her little brother Axel follows her everywhere she goes. He completely idolizes her. And when he's not following Gigi, he's following his daddy around.

Diego is a good father. Better than his own—which doesn't say much, but he swore upon Gigi's birth he would not to be a shitty parent. He grew up in a rough neighborhood with an equally rough family. He didn't have it easy growing up. Sometimes, he feels guilty that our children have so much.

"Are they spoiled?" he'll ask me every once in a while. "They never have to ask for anything."

"We can afford it," I always remind him. "Why wouldn't we give them everything we can?"

When Ava invited me to go to the bachelorette weekend, celebrating Hannah, I initially said I couldn't make it. Leaving my children, and my husband, for an entire weekend, when I always complain how it feels as if we never spend enough time with each other.

I couldn't justify it.

It was Diego who convinced me to go. He wanted me to get away and have some fun.

"I'll take care of the kids," he reassured me one late night in bed, as we were lying there, talking. Those are my favorite times. When the house is quiet and it feels like the two of us are the only ones awake in the world. We share our hopes and dreams. We listen to each other's concerns. We laugh over memories. Sometimes, we even have sex.

Okay, fine. We have sex a lot of the time, especially lately. When you've been with someone for so long, your sex life turns into stages. Sometimes you're doing it all the time, and other times, you're so busy and tired, you go through a dry spell. We're currently in a good one, and I feel so connected to him.

"You will?" My skepticism must've shown because he acted insulted.

"What? You think I can't handle it? I'm out on a field for months with thousands of spectators watching us, trying to gauge Bennett's mood and if he's going to actually throw the ball at me or not," Diego retorted.

"Playing football and taking care of our children are two very different things."

"Both amount to a lot of pressure."

I couldn't argue with that.

"I can do it," he said with a finality I didn't bother protesting.

Because I knew with that one sentence that he could.

Then Jake planned his bachelor party for the same weekend and that idea was tossed aside. My mom and my little sister Addie came to our place in Seattle and are watching the kids for us while we're both gone.

Now I'm currently in a giant bathroom with Hannah and Sophie, getting ready for our big night in, which still consists of us wearing our finest going-out dresses and doing our hair and makeup as if we're about to participate in a photoshoot.

"I wish I had dark hair," Sophie says, her gaze finding mine in the mirror's reflection. "I feel so pale and washed-out next to you."

I scan Sophie with her perfect dancer's body and her bright blonde hair that looks like spun gold. She's wearing a champagne-colored dress that is short and clingy, and she stands so straight and tall—she's stunning. "Please. You're absolutely gorgeous."

"Both of you, shut it," Hannah mutters, leaning in close to apply light pink gloss to her lips. "I should've never sat out in the sun so long."

"You wore sunscreen, right?" I ask, concern kicking in. I've turned into such a mom, even with my friends.

Hannah nods. "Oh yeah. You saw me keep applying it, right? Still got sunburned. And look at all the freckles on my face." Hannah scrunches up her nose and sticks her tongue out at her reflection.

"I think the freckles are cute," Sophie chirps.

"And right before my wedding too. They'll show up in all the photos," Hannah whines.

"Jake loves all versions of you," I remind her. "Freckles or no freckles."

"Oh, I always have freckles. I just have even more if I sit out in the sun too long." Hannah caps her lip gloss and drops it back into her cosmetics bag, frowning once more at her reflection. "I should've worn a hat like Ava's."

"That hat was ridiculous," I say without hesitation, making us bust up laughing.

Seriously. The brim on that thing almost shaded Ava's entire face, which I guess was the point.

Maybe she was the smartest one out of all of us, wearing that hat.

"Be honest, guys. Do I look ridiculous?" Hannah asks.

Sophie and I turn our full attention onto our friend. She's wearing a short white dress with thin shoulder straps that crisscross in the back. The fabric is covered with iridescent sequins that shimmer and sparkle with her every movement. Even when she breathes.

The both of us stare at her without saying a word for so long, Hannah gets agitated.

"That's it. I'm changing out of this." She starts for her bedroom, but Sophie grabs her hand, stopping her.

"No, you're perfect. You look stunning, Hannah. I just—I couldn't find the words to describe how beautiful you are." Sophie sends me a frantic look that clearly says, *help me out here.*

"I feel the same way." My chest is tight, and my eyes are starting to well up. Oh God. "I just—you're beautiful, Hannah. That white dress is perfection. You could walk down the aisle in it, it's so pretty."

"You guys." Hannah looks from me to Sophie and back to me again. "You both look like you could cry right now."

I wipe at the corner of my eye, capturing the moisture there. "I'm not crying."

"You're so crying!" Hannah points at me, her own blue eyes filling with tears. "Damn it, Jos! Don't ruin my makeup!" She waves her hands in front of her face, as if that could stop the tears from flowing.

We all laugh, and I notice that Sophie dabs at her eyes real quick too.

"Wait until you're in your wedding gown," Sophie says with a sigh. "We'll all be a blubbering mess."

"No crying allowed before the wedding," Hannah warns her best friend. "Fable hired out an entire glam squad, or whatever you want to call it, to help us all get ready. We can't ruin our makeup with uncontrollable crying."

I smile brightly, looking to change the subject and get us moving. Plus, I'm hungry. "Come on. Let's go downstairs," I suggest.

Everyone else is waiting on us in the living room, and they're just as glammed out as we are. I'm wearing a pale pink strapless dress I wore to a bachelorette party last summer for one of the player's now wife. I thought it was the perfect dress to bring for the weekend, and I'm glad I did. There is so much bling and black and sparkle, and I can't deny it.

We all look pretty damn fabulous.

"Please tell me we're having a photoshoot," Sophie says the moment she sees all of us standing together. "We must capture this moment in time, and not just with our phones."

"There's a photographer waiting outside in the back yard for us right now," Autumn says with a smile. She's adorable as ever in a shimmery sleek gold dress that clings to her curves.

"Wait—you hired a photographer?" Hannah squeals.

"You bet I did. I wish I would've hired one for us last

night too. We were dressed to kill," Autumn says, all of us nodding our agreement.

We're about to head out to the back yard when my phone rings and I see it's my husband.

"Let me take this really quick," I tell them as I answer the call. "Hey, babe."

"I miss you. I didn't touch the stripper," is how Diego greets me.

I laugh, watching as everyone exits the house and goes into the back yard. "Oh, trust me, I wasn't upset about that."

"Everyone else has been fielding calls from their women and I realized I was the only one who didn't hear from mine." He hesitates. "You're not mad, are you?"

"Absolutely not," I say without hesitation. "I trust you. I love you."

He grows quiet, seeming to absorb my words. I like that they still mean something to him, even after all of these years together. "I love you too."

"You having fun?" I ask.

"I'm tired from staying out too late last night and then we golfed this afternoon. The Arizona sun is intense. I'm sunburned, and everyone was giving me shit because I'm Mexican, and we're not supposed to burn."

I laugh. "You usually tan more than you burn."

"Yeah, well, Phoenix is a whole other kind of sun." He chuckles. "I'm still hungover yet we're going out again tonight. But I'm having a great time."

"Good. I'm glad."

"How about you?"

"Lots of female bonding, drinking and hanging out in the sun." Considering we live in Seattle, and we're both spending the weekend in a sunny locale, I know we're soaking it up. "We're having dinner made by our personal chef tonight. He brought in an entire crew to take care of us."

"Sounds fancy as fuck."

I burst out laughing. "This entire weekend has been fancy as fuck."

"Same. Jake knows how to spend money."

"So do his sisters. This is so not Hannah's style. But she's loving it. I can tell."

"Can't wait for the wedding."

"Maui, here we come." I clutch my phone close, smiling. "I miss you."

"Miss you too. See you tomorrow?"

"You know it." I smile, my stomach fluttering at his words, at the sound of his deep voice. I still get butterflies after all this time being with him, and I love it. "Love you."

"Love you too, baby. Don't get in too much trouble."

CHAPTER 9

HANNAH

A fifteen-minute photo session with me and the girls turned into a half hour. Once we were done posing endlessly around the pool, a couple of servers came outside with trays full of appetizers and drinks, including one called the Hannah Cabana. It's fruity and fresh and loaded with alcohol.

By the time dinner is served, I'm starting in on my third one.

"Girl, you better slow down," Gracie says, eyeing me from across the table. "You don't want to get carried away."

"It's my weekend to party." I raise my glass toward her in a mock toast. "I'm having a good time."

"You're going to be drunk and sloppy by the time dinner is over." She raises her brows, and while I don't see judgment on her face, I do see concern.

But, come on, I never do this kind of thing.

I offer her a faint smile and choose to ignore the warning. I can handle partying hard this weekend. That's the point, right? It's a once in a lifetime celebration of my upcoming wedding. I'm allowed to live it up and have some fun.

And we all know it's hard for Gracie to relax on this trip because she's pregnant and physically miserable. She was complaining to us earlier about her back pain and the constant need to pee. The endless baby hiccups and heartburn she's suffering through on the daily and how she can't ever seem to get comfortable. Plus, there's the lack of sleep and brain fog and constipation and her nonstop worry about childbirth.

It's a lot. She wasn't telling us that stuff for shock value. More like she was calmly listing her ailments, and while she's grateful to be having a baby and that she got pregnant fairly easily, she also says it's hard work.

Not for the faint of heart, I believe was her exact quote.

I'm not sure if I'm up to it. At least, not yet. Maybe not ever? I don't know.

We've discussed starting a family a few times and our answer is always, yeah. Maybe later.

Fine by me.

What if I never want children? I'm content right now, painting and selling my work. I want to expand my business. I want to be in more galleries, have more showings. I want my art to become even more valuable, and I want collectors demanding more of it. I don't need to become world famous or anything like that—Jake has that part handled, thanks to the Super Bowl win—but I would love to leave a mark in the art world.

I'm young, all the gallerists who I speak with tell me that I have lots of time and that the way I think and feel will shift and change as I grow older. My art will too. I'll have different periods, they tell me, and I know what they're talking about. I've studied enough art history to understand what they're saying.

But I can't help but be eager to make my mark now

though. When it comes to my work, I'm impatient. I see Jake's success and I want a small part of that, just for me.

Then I remember all the years he's put into football and how hard he's worked—with his father's help, that cannot be denied—and I realize that I do need to put in the time.

I must pay my dues.

My career plans are all forgotten tonight though. The more I drink, the friendlier I feel. I'm hugging on my friends and telling them how much I love them. Raving over the appetizers and how they're the best I've ever eaten. When we're finally allowed back inside, I can't stop gushing over the table settings. Lush pink and white flowers fill the center and the glasses are this pale, etched pink. It's all so beautiful and was chosen just for me...

My heart is full.

"Speech, speech!" They all yell after the third course has been served and our drink glasses are full. I rise to my feet, teetering on my heels, and I smile at everyone sitting at this table. Most I've known since I was a teen. Some are newer friends. All of them are dear to me.

"Thank you for throwing this bachelorette party for me," I start. "It means so much that you could all take the time out of your busy lives to be here with me this weekend. I love all of you so much, and consider myself lucky to have such a great friend group."

A few of them make aww noises and I laugh.

"Here's to marriage. To Maui. To Jake. To all the Callahans. And to all of you." I raise my glass. "Thank you, guys. For everything!"

They raise their glasses in my direction, and we all drink, even Gracie, who has a tiny sip of Hayden's drink. We all yell at her to put the drink down, and she does so reluctantly.

By the time dessert is served—lime sorbet, made of limes

straight out of Key West—Autumn and Ava have disappeared from the table.

"Where are the Callahan sisters?" I ask, suspiciously.

Within seconds, Autumn and Ava appear, pushing a cart laden with beautifully wrapped gifts. So many gifts I gasp out loud.

"Are those all for me?"

They wheel the cart over to me, matching smiles on their faces. "We figured while we were all together, we needed to throw you a bridal shower too! So we asked everyone to bring a gift," Autumn explains.

"A sexy gift," Ava adds with a smirk.

My face goes hot as I take in the beautifully wrapped presents, thinking of what they're hiding.

Oh dear.

My friends give me so much gorgeous lingerie I wonder if I'll ever be able to wear it all. And it's all expensive.

"Tell Jake not to rip it," Hayden says when I open the beautiful silk and lace nightgown she gave me from La Perla.

"Ugh, please stop talking about my brother ripping clothing." Ava sticks her fingers in her ears, making everyone laugh.

Gracie gives me edible underwear and body lotion.

"The cinnamon stuff is hot. Don't put it on his junk," is her warning, which makes me wonder if Caleb had a reaction to the lotion.

Don't really want the details so I leave it alone.

Jocelyn gives me a set of "toys"—a feather tickler, a tiny leather whip and some handcuffs.

"What is this? Gear for her secret 'Fifty Shades' room?" Sophie asks before she dissolves into endless giggles.

Someone has clearly had too much to drink.

Once all the gifts have been unwrapped, it's time for us to

go outside for "the show," as Autumn calls it. I know exactly what they're referring to.

The male strippers they've hired.

Unable to help myself, I call my husband-to-be. He picks up, and I can tell from the loud background noise that he's at a busy restaurant or bar.

"What are you doing?" I ask him.

"Eating dinner. What are you doing?"

"Thinking about the edible underwear I got as a gift."

He goes silent. Pretty sure I can hear Caleb and Jackson in the background, shit-talking.

"You've got nothing to say about that?"

Jake clears his throat. "Who gave you edible underwear?"

"Hey, Gracie's worn some before!" Caleb bellows.

"Gracie," I answer.

"Figures." Jake's voice lowers. "What else did you get?"

"Lots of beautiful lingerie. Some of it is downright scandalous." Like the set Autumn got me, which was surprising. Little scraps of expensive black lace that would barely cover me.

"Can't wait to see it."

"You're not allowed to rip it."

"Who said anything about ripping it?" He sounds amused.

"Hayden. She said it's too expensive to rip."

"Good thing I make a lot of money," Jake drawls.

"Hmm, maybe I will let you rip it off my body." I laugh.

"You been drinking, Banana?"

My entire body goes warm. He hasn't called me that in a while. I half blame it on him being with the people he used to hang out with all the time when we were in high school. "Maybe."

"Don't have too much fun with those strippers tonight," he warns.

"I don't care about male strippers," I reassure him, earning a frown from Hayden and Sophie. "I only care about you."

"Who are you talking to?" Sophie asks me.

"Jake."

"Oh my God, get off the phone with him." Hayden stalks toward me and tries to take my phone—and eventually succeeds. "Hey, Jake. Your wife-to-be has to go. Yeah, the strippers are almost here. Don't worry. We're all on a strict 'look but don't touch' policy over here, okay? Tell your homeboys they've got nothing to worry about."

She ends the call before he can say anything. Before I can tell him that I love him and I miss him. When she hands me my phone, I immediately send him a text.

Me: **Hayden stole my phone and then ended the call when I wanted to tell you goodbye.**

Me: **I love you. I miss you.**

He answers immediately.

Jake: **I love you too. Can't wait to see you tomorrow.**

Me: **Same. Have fun tonight.**

Jake: **You too. But not TOO much fun.**

He then sends me a bunch of winking face emojis.

Smiling, I clutch my phone to my chest, then let out a squeal when I see three handsome men in the back yard, every single one of them wearing police uniforms.

"Oh no! Looks like we're busted!" Ava yells, slapping her cheeks with her hands before she heads outside.

Shaking my head, I chase after her, eager to check out the show.

CHAPTER 10

JAKE

 hree weeks later

"Looks like this is it," I say as I turn right and start down the long driveway that leads to the house my parents booked for the week. "Damn, we're right on the ocean."

"The compound is on ten acres of oceanfront property," Hannah says. "And when I say compound, I mean it. There are two houses—or is it three? And so many bedrooms. We could probably go for days without seeing someone if we wanted to."

"Thank God we like everyone that'll be there," I mutter as I follow my father, who's driving the car ahead of us. He's got Mom with him, along with my little brother Beck and his girlfriend, Addie.

Wonder if those two are sharing a room? Probably not. They're still in high school for God's sake.

I glance over at Hannah and think of all the things we were doing when we were seniors in high school and realize my baby brother, the one who used to run around the house and destroy everything in his path, is probably now getting some on the regular. With Jocelyn's little sister.

Ha. Life is wild.

"I sent you a link a few weeks ago so you could check it out," Hannah says, her gaze glued to the window as she takes it all in. I can't blame her.

The locale is beautiful. The ocean is spread out before us, as far as the eye can see. And there are islands in the distance. The sun is shining, there are little white puffy clouds in the sky, and the wind is blowing through the palm trees that line the drive.

"I don't think I got it," I say absently, focused on the house before us. It's massive, with a huge staircase leading up to the double front doors, lush vegetation and smooth, green grass. "It's like a hotel."

"I texted the link to you."

"Guess I forgot to check it out." I don't even mind. Makes everything that's here more of a surprise.

I eventually park the Ford Bronco we rented in the circular driveway, right in front of the steps that lead to the house. A man comes out to assist us, taking our luggage and putting it on a cart, like we're at a hotel, just like I said.

"What do you think?" my father asks as he approaches us, his arms spread out and a giant smile on his face. "Pretty nice, huh?"

"It's beautiful." Hannah looks around, her gaze landing on the bubbling fountain in the center of the circular drive. "I can't wait to see this place at night. There are lights everywhere."

"It's a beautiful location," Mom says with a fond smile as she stops to stand next to my father. "Only the best for you two and your special weekend."

"Gonna do something like this for me when I get

married?" Beck asks, his brows shooting up. He's standing right next to her and he towers over our short mother. She's barely five-foot-one and Beck is over six-four. He's wider than me too.

Freaking aggravates me, that my little brother is bigger than I am. I try not to focus on it, but deep down, I hate it.

Which makes me sound like a petty bitch, so I never voice my opinion on the matter.

"I don't even want to think about you getting married right now," Mom says, shaking her head. "You're only eighteen."

"Don't worry. We're gonna go to college first. Once we graduate, then we'll get married." The confidence in my brother's voice is unreal.

"You really think you've got it all figured out?"

Beck turns his focus to Addie, who's running over to the car that just pulled up behind us, Jocelyn and Diego inside. A faint smile curves his lips, his gaze returning to mine. "Hell yeah. She's the one. Didn't you feel the same way about Hannah when you were my age?"

Sort of. Not really. I was just…living in the moment. Especially at first. I wasn't looking that far into my future.

It was only when we got accepted to different colleges that I realized just how important she was to me—and how I didn't want to lose her.

"Does she know you two are getting married?" I ask my brother, keeping the focus on him.

Beck shrugs, as easygoing as he always is. "She's gotta sense it, you know? I mean, I know what I want, and that's her. Pretty sure she wants the same thing. Meaning, me."

Hannah wraps her arms around my middle and rests her head against my chest, a dreamy smile on her face—directed right at my brother. "You two are the absolute sweetest."

"My romantic almost-wife." I drop a kiss on the top of her head.

"Okay, enough chatting. Come on, you guys. Let's go get everyone's rooms arranged," Mom says, waving her hand and indicating she wants us to follow her.

We fall into line behind her as she leads us through the house on a quick tour, Hannah's hand locked in mine, her head turning this way and that as she takes it all in. Dad stays out in front of the house, waiting so he can greet the rest of our guests when they arrive.

Always the leader, my father. Mom is the nurturer, wanting to make sure everyone is taken care of and happy.

I definitely lucked out in the parent department.

As we move through the house, I'm in complete awe—and I've seen a lot of fancy shit in my time. The main house is all open space and giant windows. Huge lanais—outdoor porches—that are part of the living space, with overstuffed furniture and views for days. You can see nothing but the ocean from the back of the house, plus a couple of islands in the distance.

"That's Molokai," Mom says, pointing to one of the islands.

When I was younger, we'd come to Maui for vacations a lot. And most of them were spent on this side of the island. We'd stay at one of the hotels on La Haina and hang out by the pool with Mom or snorkel in the ocean with Dad. We'd feed the turtles and scrape up our hands and knees on the boogie boards when we tried to surf. Beck was too small at first, so it would always just be me, Autumn and Ava, and damn, we made a lot of good memories on this island.

I'm glad Hannah and I are getting married here. Now we're creating more memories. A new generation of them.

"You guys get your own guest house," Mom says as we walk outside. She points toward a smaller version of the house we just exited. "It's right there. Has the absolute best views."

"I can't wait," Hannah says, her voice almost trembling with excitement.

"There are so many bedrooms in this place, it's unreal." Mom casts a glance in Beck and Addie's direction. "Beck, you're sharing with your cousin, and Addie you'll share a room with my brother's girls."

Beck rolls his eyes. "Come on—"

Addie jabs him in the ribs with her elbow, effectively shutting him up.

Smart move. He doesn't need to gripe to Mom about not sharing a room with Addie. Sometimes he acts older than he really is.

"When do Uncle Owen and Aunt Chelsea get here?" I ask. They're coming with their three kids: Knox, Ruby and Blair. Knox is in college and is an excellent football player.

No surprise there. Our family tree is full of football players.

"Their plane arrives…" Mom checks her phone for the time. "Soon, actually."

"My mom arrives tonight," Hannah says.

"I know. We met for lunch a few days ago and discussed the wedding," Mom says.

"You did?" Hannah sounds shocked, which is funny considering our moms have become closer over the years because of us. For whatever reason, Hannah seems to find that hard to believe.

Mom nods, her gaze going to Addie. "Your mom was with us, too."

"She told me." Addie smiles. "It's kind of cool, how you're all becoming friends."

"Becoming?" Mom lifts her brows. "We're already friends.

And it's a natural progression, you know? Some of us are becoming family in a couple of days."

I tug on Hannah's hand, and she glances up at me, her brows drawn together. "Let's go check out our place."

She smiles. "Okay."

We excuse ourselves and head for the house that's ours for the next week. As we get closer, I see it sits on the farthest point of the property, closer to the cliffs, which means we're the closest to the ocean. The sound of the waves crashing against the rocks is louder here and I stop for a moment, studying the view, my hand still entwined with Hannah's.

"It's gorgeous," she murmurs, her gaze on the water.

I glance over at her. "Almost as gorgeous as you."

She sends me a look. "Sweet talker."

"I'm being real with you right now, Banana. Don't stomp on my game." I pull her into my arms as she protests, a laugh escaping her right before I press my mouth to hers. "I can't wait to marry you."

Hannah wraps her arms around me, her hands roaming up and down my back. "I can't wait to marry you too."

We kiss for long, tongue-filled minutes, right there in front of our guest house, forgetting about everyone and everything that's happening around us. I get lost in her taste, the feel of her against me, the murmuring sounds of pleasure she makes while I keep kissing her.

Is it always going to feel like this? No. I know that for a fact. We've had our ups and downs, but the downs are never so bad that I contemplate ending things with her. Hell no.

I never want to lose her. She means too much to me.

"We should go inside," she murmurs sometime later, once we break apart to catch our breath. "Check out our house."

"Check out our bed." My hand lands on her ass, giving it a squeeze.

"Are you going to have sex on the brain for the entirety of our stay here or what?" She lifts a single brow.

I nod. What's the point in denying it? "We're on our honeymoon. Isn't that how it's supposed to be?"

"Yeah, it is, which is a good thing, considering I'm feeling the same way."

I smack her ass and she laughs, just before she extracts herself from my arms and darts toward the house.

Chuckling, I follow after her.

CHAPTER 11

AUTUMN

"**W**ant to see the outfits Jaden and Luna are wearing for the wedding?" I ask.

My husband and I are in the main bedroom of our two-room suite, unpacking our suitcases and situating ourselves for the week. Our twins are with my mom and dad, who are already in the pool with them.

Our babies are eighteen months old and they are a handful. When they were first born, I wanted to take care of them on my own. I didn't need a nanny, I kept telling Ash. I learned from the best, and I could totally do this.

After a while, I became overwhelmed. Once they started to walk, forget it. I was chasing them everywhere. Crying. Exhausted. During football season, I started to feel completely isolated. So alone. Until my husband finally had enough and said one day, "Fuck this. We're hiring a nanny. It doesn't make you less of a mother if you need help."

My life has completely changed since Laura came into our lives. She's around my mother's age, has adult children and is so good with babies, it's not even funny. Our twins adore her.

So do I.

Where we're staying here in Maui is so unbelievably beautiful, I can't get over it. My parents call it the compound. The estate is so large, the wedding is being held here too. Out on the lawn, overlooking the ocean.

It's happening in two days, and I can't wait.

"Our children are getting dressed up for the wedding?" Ash has his back to me as he hangs up his clothes in the closet.

An irritated sound leaves me. Sometimes, my husband forgets important details. "They're actually in the wedding, Ash. Remember?"

He turns to face me, chuckling. "Really? Your brother and Hannah want to take that risk, huh?"

"What do you mean?" I rest my hands on my hips, vaguely offended.

"They're going to be chasing those little buggers everywhere. They don't ever stay in one spot and you know it."

"Kenzie and Rhett are in it too," I add.

Ash breaks into full-blown laughter. "It's going to be a major disaster then."

"Asher." He must hear the irritation in my tone because the laughter dies. "It's going to be meaningful, having our children participate in my brother's wedding. Jake and Hannah asked me if they could."

"More like Hannah asked you, but whatever." He resumes unpacking his suitcase.

"You want to see the outfits?" I ask again, trying to tamp down my irritation.

I've been a little on edge lately, and I don't know why. Things are going well for us. Ash's NFL career is still going strong—he just signed another four-year contract for an ungodly amount of money. Thanks to that contract, and knowing Ash is in a more permanent place, we just bought a new home and are moving in about a month. Our children are thriving. I'm making friends with the other players' wives, getting closer to the ones who have children so we can compare notes. I feel close to my family as well. The bachelorette party we threw for Hannah a few weeks ago was a smashing success, and we all had so much fun.

Now we're here on Maui, together again, and ready to celebrate for a week. I've been looking forward to this trip for a long time.

So why am I irritated right now?

Ash turns to face me once more, his dark eyes knowing. I'm sure he can tell I'm annoyed. "Definitely, babe. Show me what you got."

I pull out the little mini suit for our son and the fluffy white dress made of tulle for our daughter. They're on tiny hangers and I turn them this way and that, letting my husband get a full look at them. "Aren't they adorable?"

"Really cute," he says with a nod. "Are they actually walking down the aisle?"

"Something like that." I'm purposely vague, because we have a plan for them, and we all think it's going to be great.

I'm hanging the outfits up in my closet when Ash says, "Hey." He comes up behind me, settling his hands on my shoulders and I lean into him. "You all right?"

A sigh leaves me. "I think I'm stressed."

"Why?" He presses his mouth to my temple in a soft kiss. "Tell me what's up."

"I don't know. Things are changing, and it's all happening so fast." I pause for a moment, savoring the feel of my husband's fingers in my hair. "I'm kind of stressed."

"I'll help you with the move. I've got nothing going."

"Until you start training."

"That's not for a while still." He slips his arms around my middle and holds me close. "I know I'm busy and I leave a lot of the family stuff on you. I hate that."

"I'm used to it. I witnessed it happening between my mom and dad, you know."

"Doesn't make it right." He pushes my hair aside and drops a soft kiss on my neck. "Whatever you need when we get back home, I'll get you. I want to help you, Autumn. I love you. We're in this together."

"I know." Just hearing him say that lowers my stress level. Even if I don't need him for whatever I'm dealing with, just knowing that he's there and available makes me feel better. "I need to hire a moving company."

"You haven't done that already?" He sounds surprised.

"I've been busy helping with this wedding." It's true. Mom and I have done a lot of planning for this event, though Hannah also hired a wedding planner that lives on the island. "And the kids, and Hannah's bachelorette weekend…"

"Say no more." He turns me so I'm facing him, his gaze meeting mine. "I'll call around and find a moving company when we get home."

I smile faintly. "Thank you. That would help a lot. One less thing I have to deal with."

Ash kisses me, his lips lingering, and I respond, winding my arms around his neck. His hands slip down my back, until they're resting on my butt and I shift closer to him, savoring his touch. "I am always here for you, baby. I don't ever want you to feel like you have too much going on and I'm not helping you."

"You have a lot going on as well," I remind him, thinking of that big contract and what it means. How much the coaches and owners expect from him. There's a lot of pressure on my husband, and I know that while he was happy my

76

brother and his team won the Super Bowl, he wished that could've been his team who did it.

"I do." He dips his head, his forehead against mine. "I can handle it though."

"I can handle it too," I say softly, pressing my hands against his firm chest. "We're in this together, right?"

He smiles. "Always have been."

Before I can say anything else, he kisses me deep, his tongue tangling with mine. I slide my hands up, until my arms are around his neck and my hands are in his hair. His hands are wandering, slipping beneath the hem of my dress. I can feel him grow harder, and when his fingers trail up the outside of my thigh—

There's a rapid knock on the door.

"Jesus," Ash mutters, clearing his throat. He raises his voice to ask, "What's up?"

"Sorry to bug, but Mom needs one of you out at the pool. Or both of you. Says she has something to show you," Beck yells from the other side of the door.

A giggle leaves me when Ash curses under his breath. "We'll be right out!"

"Hurry up, Mom says. It might not last long." With that last statement, we hear Beck take off down the hall.

Ash slowly releases his grip on me, his hands sliding along my body, leaving tingles in their wake. "It's going to be like this the entire week we're here, huh?"

"Maybe." More like probably.

He shakes his head, his mouth curved up. "Better go see what's going on with the kids."

"Mom probably taught them how to swim."

My husband's brows shoot up in surprise. "Really? That fast?"

I shrug. "It's amazing what that woman can do when she sets her mind to it."

"I feel the same way about you." He kisses the tip of my nose.

I melt at his words, and I swear I feel tears prick the corners of my eyes. "I love you."

"Love you too. More than you can possibly know."

CHAPTER 12

HANNAH

*O*ur wedding day dawns bright and sunny. Not a single cloud in the sky. I wake up to the sound of the wind rattling the palm trees closest to our guest house, snuggled up close to my very naked husband-to-be. I also happen to be naked.

Last night was one I'll never forget. We ran through our wedding rehearsal, and while we had a few hiccups, all of them involving the coordination of the children, for the most part, it went smoothly. After we ran through the ceremony a couple of times, we had an amazing dinner surrounded by family and friends. Our dinner was a luau with delicious food, and while we ate, there was entertainment with hula and fire dancers. During dessert, there were fireworks. There was way too much alcohol flowing, which led to sappy speeches, dancing, and at one point, even karaoke. Eli was the best at it—he wouldn't stop singing, actually. Ava finally had to drag him away around two in the morning, so they could get some sleep.

Who knew Eli had such a great singing voice? He wouldn't let Jackson do karaoke, which was hilarious.

Though Eli chose one of Jackson's songs. That one he wrote for Ellie called "Pink."

Yeah, that was kind of weird yet funny. Ellie kept yelling for Eli to stop and everyone was hysterically laughing. Our parents had already retired for the night and took the younger kids with them. Even Diego and Jocelyn's kids. Everyone got a reprieve, and we acted like teenagers, partying all night long.

I think Beck enjoyed it the most out of all of us. He's never really "partied" with us before, and I think after all these years of feeling like the little kid who got left behind, he finally feels part of the gang.

Which is fine by me. I love Jake's little brother. He's the sweetest.

"You awake?" Jake's voice is so low, I almost don't hear him.

Tilting my head back, I smile up at him. "Good morning."

"Morning." He kisses me, apparently not bothered by morning breath. "Happy wedding day."

A giddy sensation rises up in me and I can't contain the grin that grows on my face. "Happy wedding day."

"You ready for the chaos?"

"Don't say that," I chastise him. "It's going to go smoothly."

"Oh, the wedding is going to be great, but you know there will be chaos as we get ready."

We hear the sound of hammering in the distance.

"What is that?" I ask.

"Who knows. I'm sure they're constructing something for the ceremony."

"Maybe they're putting together the flower arbor." That flower bill for the original wedding about sent me over the edge, but the one for this ceremony is no better. Flowers are really expensive.

Oh well. We can afford it. Fable reassured me I shouldn't worry. We're doing this right. Those were her exact words.

"Isn't there some sort of superstition where the couple isn't supposed to be together on their wedding day?" Jake asks me. "It's bad luck, right?"

"Well, yeah, but come on. That's impossible. We're not even getting married until later this afternoon."

"True."

"I don't believe in that sort of stuff," I add. "We make our own luck."

"Most of the time, but there are things we can't control."

"Jake." I scoot over, so I'm basically sprawled on top of him, and his hands automatically land on my bare butt. "With this wedding, we're making our own luck. Yes, we can't control the many crazy children that are here, but we've got this."

His smile is lazy; his face covered in scruff. Over the last couple of weeks, he's let a beard grow in because he doesn't feel like shaving, and I have to admit…

I like it. A lot.

His mom was giving him grief over the scruff last night, but he told her straight up that I liked it, which made her stop complaining.

My handsome, bearded husband. I reach for his face, cupping his cheek as I smile at him. "You get better looking with time, I swear."

"You do too. I remember the first time I really noticed you, reading your book at lunch." He laughs.

I scowl. "You were offended I turned down your offer to wear your jersey."

"I was. I couldn't believe you turned me down."

"I figured you were trying to set me up and make me look stupid." My insecurities back then were crushing sometimes.

81

"I kind of was." His expression is pained. "Diego and I back in the day—we were shits."

"Yeah, you were." I kiss him. "Thank God for rational Tony."

"And Caleb," he adds.

"Please. Caleb was never rational."

"True." It's his turn to kiss me. "Remember how much I hated Eli?"

I nod. "And now he's your brother-in-law."

"He still annoys me sometimes." Jake frowns. "He's just so…"

"Full of it?" I supply for him.

"Full of shit," Jake corrects. "Though he's a damn good singer. Who knew?"

"We're always too busy listening to Jackson."

We reminisce for a while, until we start getting text messages from various people. My mother. His. Ava and Autumn. Diego is looking for Jake because he's the best man and I think he feels responsible for rounding up the groom. Sophie sends me a quick text just to check in.

"We need to get going," I finally say, after checking my phone for what feels like the hundredth time, though I'm exaggerating.

"Let me savor you for a few minutes longer." He pulls me into him, snuggling me close, and I rest my head on his firm shoulder, breathing in his familiar scent. "We've been together a long time."

"I know."

"And now I'm making you my wife."

I like how he phrases that. "I can't wait."

"I love you, Hannah Walsh, soon-to-be Callahan."

I like how that sounds too. "I love you too."

"I have something for you."

I glance up at him. "You do?"

He nods, then rolls over on his side, reaching over to the nightstand and opening the drawer. He pulls a box out and turns to face me, holding it out. "For you."

I take it from him with trembling fingers, staring at it for a moment before I lift my gaze to his. "What is it?"

He flicks his chin. "Open it and find out."

Curious, I slowly lift the lid to find a necklace on a delicate gold chain, two tiny diamond circles interlocked. "Oh, this is beautiful."

"It's us," he says. "The two of us, locked together forever."

His words, the sincerity in his voice, make tears immediately spring to my eyes. I glance up at him, my vision blurry. "Jake..."

"Wear it when you walk down the aisle, okay? I showed it to my mom and she said it would work with your dress."

"Even if it didn't, I'd still wear the necklace." I close the lid, clutching the box in my hand as I hug him. "I love it so much. Thank you."

"Thank you for doing me the honor of becoming my wife," he whispers in my ear. "I still can't believe this is happening."

"Took you long enough," I whisper, making him laugh. "Seriously, Jake. Everyone wondered at one point if we were actually ever going to get married."

"Gotta keep them guessing, babe, you know?" He smiles and I kiss him, because he's hard to resist when he looks at me like that.

This man who used to be an angry, arrogant boy. Who used to think he owned the world and everyone in it, and somehow believed they still owed him. He had such a chip on his shoulder when we first met, but as time went on, with me, he became so patient. So sweet and thoughtful and determined. And now he's the strong and loving man I'm going to marry today.

I'm the luckiest woman in the world, and while I know I created my own luck with a lot of things in my life, fate handed me Jake Callahan one random day at the beginning of our senior year, and we haven't looked back since.

"Well, they all know what's happening now," I tease him. "You're finally making it legal."

"You don't need a legal piece of paper proving my love for you, do you, Banana?" His fingers drift across my cheek, making me shiver.

"No. But I have to admit, I'm really excited to finally become Hannah Callahan." I kiss him, and he kisses me back, murmuring he loves me against my lips.

All feels right in the world.

CHAPTER 13

AVA

$\mathcal{W}$e're waiting to walk out for the wedding ceremony and standing in a line, Hannah at the back of it with her brother. For some unexplained reason, I feel nervous.

Even a little shaky.

Our children are directly behind us, Kenzie keeping watch over her little brother, though I just said that to make her feel like a big girl. She's pretty good at taming him though. She gets firm with him, just like a little mama, and that tells me she's watching me far more closely than I ever thought.

Scary.

Eli grabs my hand and hooks my arm through his as we hear the music cue up. "You ready?"

Nodding, I study his handsome profile, those hazel eyes twinkling at me as usual. Like he's full of mischief and can't be trusted. "You're not going to do anything crazy today, are you?"

"During the ceremony? No way." He makes a dismissive

noise, like I should have more faith in him, but come on. It's Eli—and my brother. "I do have a speech planned for the reception though."

Oh God. "Nothing too inappropriate, okay? There's a lot of family here."

Well, not really. I'm just saying that.

"I've got it handled, princess." He pats my hand. "Trust me on that."

That's not reassuring at all.

Glancing over my shoulder, I smile at my babies, who are hand in hand staring up at me. "You guys ready? It's almost time."

Kenzie nods. "I'm so ready, Mommy."

"Yes!" Rhett yells, his lisp making it sound more like 'yeth.'

They both match us, Kenzie, in a pale blue dress that's made of the same fabric as our bridesmaid dresses, and Rhett, in a miniature version of the suit the groomsmen are wearing. Diego is the best man, and Sophie is the maid of honor. The rest of the wedding party is Autumn, Jocelyn and me, along with Ash, Beck and Eli. Jake asked Caleb to participate, but he wanted to stay in the audience with his very pregnant wife, who appears ready to pop at any given moment. I'm surprised her doctor allowed her to fly to Maui.

If she has the baby while we're all here on the island, I wouldn't be shocked.

"Be good, okay?" My children nod at my request, their eyes big, their expressions solemn. "I need you to behave so everything goes like it's supposed to for Uncle Jake's wedding."

"It's important," Kenzie says, shaking Rhett's hand, like he'll understand what she's saying.

I told her exactly that last night, when we were at the wedding rehearsal. I gave her a little speech about the ceremony and how much it means to her aunt and uncle, and how important it is for them to do what they need to do. Kenzie is all about wanting to make a good impression, and she loves putting on a show when she has an audience.

Being a flower girl is right in her wheelhouse.

"Be careful with the basket," I advise as my mom makes her way toward us. She looks beautiful in a pale pink dress, her once long hair now cut to just above her shoulders. Still as bright and as blonde as ever. I swear she could pass as one of our sisters. "Go with Grandma, okay? Listen to what she tells you."

"Come on, Kenz." Mom takes Kenzie's hand and leads them to the front of the line. Our children will walk down the aisle first, Kenzie scattering rose petals in front of her while Rhett accompanies her. Next will be Jaden and Luna, who are riding in a toy car down the aisle that Caleb will control with a remote.

It's so freaking cute. Such a fun detail.

Then the wedding party will head out. Jake's already standing out there, waiting for the ceremony to start, looking nervous with his hands clutched in front of him. There are white flowers literally dripping from the arbor that stands tall behind him, and there are also flowers lining the white aisle we're all walking down. Gentle music plays from a string quartet and the weather is just perfect. Not too hot, not too windy.

Like everything settled down, just for this moment.

"This is so weird," Eli mutters, and I glance over at him with a frown.

"What are you talking about?"

"I can't believe I'm in Jake Callahan's wedding." Eli shakes his head. "I hated that guy."

"You don't hate him anymore." I pause. "Do you?"

87

"Hell no. Not really. Only when he's winning the Super Bowl." The pained look on my husband's face is still fresh. He hates that he lost to Jake in the playoffs, and I can't blame him.

"At least we kept it in the family?"

"True." Eli nods, his arm tightening around mine. "Still blows my mind sometimes, though. That he's part of my family, when we used to hate each other's guts."

"I think it's sweet." I press my head against my husband's shoulder, readjusting my bouquet of white flowers before I pull away from him, though our arms remain linked.

Slowly but surely, we're all heading down the aisle, and once the kids walk down—they did great, and everyone oohs and aahhhs over the remote-controlled car—it's Jocelyn and Beck who walk out before us.

"Ready?" Eli asks me, just as we're about to head out.

I nod and smile, and then we're leaving the covered lanai and walking down the long, white cloth-covered aisle, the scent of flowers everywhere since there are so many. I smile at the people we pass, our friends and family that came for the wedding. The crowd is small, just as Hannah and Jake wanted it, and we're surrounded by those who mean the most to us. Even Eli's mom came with her boyfriend. Addie and Jocelyn's parents came as well, as did Caleb's, along with Diego's mom. Eli's brother is a guest too. Ryan just arrived on Maui earlier today, and he brought a mystery date with him?

Which we'll be getting to the bottom of during the reception.

So many people are here who had a hand in us growing up. Who guided us and did the occasional shitty thing to us too—I can't sugarcoat all of it. Some of us have struggled with our relationship with our parents. I'm lucky that I get along so well with my mom and dad, but I put them through it when I was younger. Turns out Autumn and Ash did too, though I didn't find out about that until literally last night.

Ah, family secrets. They're great, aren't they? And that one isn't even much of a doozy.

Jake also admitted last evening that he used to sneak over to Hannah's apartment all the time during their senior year, and her mom looked so shocked, I thought she'd fall off her chair. I guess it was time for confessions, though I kept my mouth shut for the most part. Ellie and I would share a look every few minutes, when something was mentioned, but we remained mum.

We were bad when the boys were seniors and we were following them everywhere. We lied a lot to our parents back then, and I really didn't want to get into that last night.

I'll confess all someday. Maybe when I'm forty?

Eli and I part ways at the end of the aisle, and I flash a smile in Jake's direction before I go take my place where the bridesmaids stand. Ash and Autumn walk down the aisle next, the both of them beaming, Ash dropping a kiss on Autumn's cheek before they part.

Ooh, I bet Eli wishes he thought of that.

Diego and Sophie are the last pair to walk down the aisle before the bride. He looks so dark and handsome in his suit, a closed-lipped smile on his face as he accompanies the ethereal Sophie. The cut of her dress is slightly different than ours, since she's the maid of honor, and she looks stunning.

If I didn't like her so much, I could be jealous of her.

The music changes, and the guests rise to their feet, turning to watch the bride appear. Within moments, Hannah is walking down the aisle on her older brother Joe's arm, the two of them smiling so big, it's almost blinding. They have similar features—even their hair color is the same, and when he delivers his sister to my brother, Joe leans in and hugs her carefully, probably not wanting to crush her dress.

And it's beautiful. Strapless and full skirted, covered with layers and layers of tulle and the cutest white-ribbon belt in the center. It's a show stopping dress, one I would've never chosen for Hannah, but when I saw her try it on, I knew.

It's the perfect gown for her.

I watch as my mother covers her mouth, her eyes damp. Hannah's mother has the same look on her face, though her tears are flowing freely. They're both overwhelmed with love, and it makes me want to tear up too.

As discreetly as I can, I dab at the corners of my eyes, offering a shaky smile at Jocelyn, who also looks ready to cry.

It's not sadness taking us over. It's all the love filling this space. The generations of people in attendance, who are here in support of Jake and Hannah and our families. This wedding is special to so many of us, and that we were able to all come together for it is just...

It's overwhelming. In the best possible way.

I don't even think I felt like this during my own wedding, which I can probably blame on being so preoccupied with every little detail. Wanting to ensure it was going to come together. I had a wedding planner, but I'm such a control freak, I couldn't help but take over and handle most of it myself. My wedding to Eli was beautiful, and while I enjoyed it, I was also exhausted. I don't remember a lot of the details of that day.

And that makes me feel a little sad.

That's why I want to enjoy this moment. Bask in the love and the sun and the smiles. The fragrant air and how our children's fine blond hair floats up with the gentle breeze. In the distance, I can hear the ocean waves, and I realize in this very moment I'm content.

Life can't get much better than this.

Watching as Jake and Hannah turn to face each other, I

smile as he takes her hands and the minister starts to speak. I can't see Hannah's face, because her back is to us, but I see all that love for her shining in my brother's eyes, and I know, without a doubt, that he's going to love her till the end of time.

And it's the sweetest thing ever.

CHAPTER 14

JAKE

"*T*he couple has written their own vows for each other and would like to share them," the minister announces.

I grip Hannah's hands in mine, noting how they tremble. She's watching me with shining eyes, and God, she's as beautiful as I've ever seen her. The wedding dress, her hair, the veil, the flowers, surrounded by everyone we love and care about...

It's a lot. Makes me want to choke up.

Clearing my throat, I stare into her blue eyes and say the words I wrote down a week ago and have been running through my head ever since.

"When I first talked to you, I never imagined we would somehow end up here. Getting married. Wanting to make you my wife. Back then, you were just some girl I barely knew, who automatically turned me down when I asked you to wear my jersey on game day."

There is polite laughter, Caleb being the loudest.

"The more I got to know you, the more I fell in love with you. To the point that I don't know how to do life without you in it. You're the most important thing to me, Hannah. Above everything else in my life. The rest of it could disappear, and I'd still be happy because I had you by my side. If you're not with me, then I don't know how to go on living."

She blinks back tears, squeezing my hands.

"I love you. You're my best friend. And now that you're going to be my wife, I'm the luckiest man in the world. You are just it for me, Banana. We've already done a lot with each other, and someday, I want to make a family with you. But right now, I'm content with having just my wife by my side, cheering me on. And when it's your turn to shine, I will continue cheering you on too. I'm your biggest fan, Hannah. I hope you know that." I glance over at the minister, who's smiling at us. "That's all I have to say."

Hannah's smile is tremulous, and she gives my hands a little shake. "You were impossible. Brash. Arrogant. Talented. Smart. Cocky. Persistent. Oh, you wouldn't let up. Once you set your sights on me, sometimes it felt as if I had no choice. I had to be with you."

I blink at her, startled by her words. They're a little...
Harsh.

"Those were my initial feelings when I first caught the eye of Jake Callahan." She smiles brightly, and seeing it eases the sting of her words. "I didn't want anything to do with him. I thought I was perfectly happy being alone, living my own life. Slowly but surely, though, he worked his way in, until I didn't know how I could go on without him. When we got accepted to colleges that weren't too far from each other, I realized that maybe we could make this work. And when he said he wanted to continue being with me after high school, I knew."

There's a pause and I smile faintly, trying to encourage her.

"I *knew* that we were going to work. I knew back then,

when we were only eighteen years old and he was my first love, that he would be my only love." Tears slide down her cheeks and I let go of her hand to wipe them away with my thumb. "I love you, Jake. I loved the boy you were, and I love the man you've become. I will love every version of you that you are, and I will do it with my entire heart. There is no other love like a Callahan love."

"You're damn right!" Dad yells from the crowd, causing Mom to shush him. Everyone then breaks into laughter, including me and my bride.

"It's true," Hannah says with a little sniff. "Your family has become my own. Your friends are mine. I'm not just loved by you, I feel as if I'm loved by all. And I'm really, really glad I took a chance on that brash, arrogant boy who pursued me during our senior year. You're the love of my life, Jacob Callahan. There is no one else for me. Just you."

Glancing around, I spot a few people who are misty-eyed. I can see tears in both of my sisters' eyes, and I hear a few sniffles. Hannah isn't crying anymore though. She looks proud. Happy.

So damn happy.

The minister launches into the standard wedding vows and we repeat the words back to him about honoring and cherishing each other till death do us part. I slip a diamond eternity band on her finger, and she slips a platinum band onto mine.

"You may now kiss the bride," the minister intones.

I pull her to me without hesitation and press my lips to hers in a long, lingering kiss. Nothing too outrageous because just as I predicted…

Our friends start making noise. Yelling and carrying on like the idiots that they are. Even my brother gets in on the action, a big ol' grin on his face.

Hannah pulls away first, laughing and shaking her head. I

grab her hand and lift it in victory, turning so that we're facing everyone.

"May I introduce Mr. and Mrs. Jacob Callahan," the minister says as we start down the aisle.

Applause erupts, and I can't stop smiling. All eyes are on us—mostly on my beautiful bride—and it feels good, to see the happiness on their faces as they clap while we walk by.

When we're back in the house, I sweep Hannah into my arms and kiss her like I mean it, only breaking the kiss when I hear Diego and Sophie's voices.

"I love you," I whisper against Hannah's lips.

She gives me a quick kiss before pulling away. "I love you too."

"You guys! Your vows! Oh my God!" Sophie runs up to Hannah and pulls her out of my arms, wrapping her up in a hug. "That was the sweetest wedding ceremony I think I've ever witnessed."

Soon the lanai is filled with our entire wedding party, including the kids. The twins, already having been taken out of the remote-control car walk in with my mom and dad, each of them carrying a toddler in their arms. It's loud and chaotic and everyone is trying to speak over each other. I glance over at my wife—what a trip, Hannah is my freaking wife—to find her already watching me, her lips curled up in a secret smile. Her cheeks and nose are dusted with freckles, as are her shoulders, and I think about how I'm going to kiss every single one of those freckles tonight.

No matter how long it takes.

"All right, all right! We need to get it together!" This comes from the photographer, who has drill-sergeant tendencies, which appear to be necessary, considering what's currently happening. "Everyone head out to the lawn! It's photo time."

"We're taking photos with the children first, right?"

Autumn asks hopefully, glancing over at her squirming children in our parents' arms.

"Absolutely," the photographer says with a nod. She's older, with graying black hair that flows to the small of her back. It's currently blowing in the breeze and she shoves a few stray strands away from her face. "Wedding party with kids first please! Let's go!"

"How long is this going to take?" I ask Hannah as I grab her hand and interlock her fingers through mine.

"Hours," Hannah says, rolling her eyes.

Alarm races through me when I realize I can't tell if she's joking or not. "You're serious?"

"I hope not. Maybe an hour?" She winces. "We took some photos before."

"Right, so did we." My stomach chooses that moment to growl. "I'm starving."

"Me too," she admits, resting her hand against her stomach.

Drawing my attention to that dress.

"Did I tell you that you're beautiful?" I let my eyes wander the length of her. All the layers of fluffy fabric—shit, I don't know what to call it—but it's pretty. Pretty sexy.

Wonder what she's got on beneath it.

"Yes, you've mentioned it a time or two." She's teasing me, her eyes sparkling. "You can say it again though."

"You're beautiful." I pull her into me, my mouth finding hers once more. "Stunning. The most gorgeous bride I've ever seen."

"I love you," she says on a sigh, slinging her arm around my neck to pull me in closer.

"Guys, stop making out. I think the photographer is going to have a coronary if you don't head out there right now," Beck says in warning as he walks past us.

Another sigh leaves Hannah and she tugs on my hand,

pulling me along. "Come on, Mr. Callahan. We need to take our wedding photos."

"Whatever you say, Mrs. Callahan," I return, grinning when she glances over her shoulder at me, pleased by me calling her that.

Mrs. Callahan. Hannah Callahan.

That has a nice ring to it.

CHAPTER 15

ELI

*D*inner is almost over and I've been anxious during the entire meal. Didn't stop me from eating though. The food was fuckin' delicious. The Callahans always know how to throw a party.

And this wedding reception doesn't disappoint.

The speeches are coming up and I need to take my moment before everything gets rolling. Leaning over my mostly empty plate, I grab my glass of champagne a server came around and poured for everyone earlier and start to rise to my feet.

My wife's hand on the crook of my arm stops me. I glance down at Ava to find her watching me, her gaze narrowed.

She has good reason to question me. I'm always trying to stir things up. It's like I can't help myself. I thought I'd grow out of this need as I got older, but nope.

I'm still up to no good.

"What are you doing?" she murmurs.

"Going to give a little speech." I reach into the pocket of my jacket and pull out a tiny slip of paper, flashing it at her. I made a few notes. Highlights, things I wanted to mention when I spoke, but I don't need the paper. Those ideas are already in my head. "Don't worry. I'll be nice."

Her expression is skeptical, her grip on me loosening, though she doesn't fully let go. "Really?"

I nod, keeping a straight face. "Promise."

Ava tugs on my arm and I dip down, my mouth finding hers in a quick kiss. I'd keep kissing her because I still can't get enough of this woman, even after all of these years. But I have a job to do.

A speech to give.

I stand up straight, glancing around at the tables spread out before us. All of our family and friends are here tonight, and it feels good. It feels right.

This is why I can't worry about what I'll say. No one will judge me. Hell, they'll laugh and know I'm just being myself.

Wait until I share my surprise at the end. They're gonna love it.

Ava grabs a spoon and taps it against her glass to try to get everyone's attention, but no one notices.

So I stick my fingers in my mouth and let a piercing whistle rip. Conversation ceases immediately and everyone turns their heads in my direction.

All eyes on me. Just the way I like it.

Smiling, I glance over at Hannah and Jake, who are sitting dead center at the wedding party table. He's watching me with wariness in his eyes, which just makes me grin wider. I love fucking with him. I don't think that will ever grow old. "I have a few things I'd like to say," I announce.

"Be nice!" This comes from Tony, making everyone laugh.

I scowl at him. "I can behave."

Caleb snort laughs, jabbing Jackson in the ribs. They're all sitting at the same table, enjoying the show.

Typical.

I glare at the both of them, and they immediately shut up,

Gracie and Ellie sending them searing looks, like they're the ones who need to behave.

Love it.

"If you would've told me back in high school that I'd be talking at Jake Callahan's wedding reception—that I would even be *attending* this guy's wedding— I would've laughed in your face. If you don't know the history between us, and I'm pretty sure most of you do, I hated the guy. Though I was always hot for his little sister." I wink at Ava, who shakes her head in response.

Amusement dances in her eyes, though. She knows I'm just speakin' the truth.

"The feeling was mutual. Jake couldn't stand me either. Once I started dating Ava, we tolerated each other—barely. He up and left after he graduated high school, but he kept coming around, visiting his family and we'd always end up spending time together. After a while, Jake started to grow on me. And then I realized—reluctantly—that I actually liked the fu—guy."

More laughter at my near miss. I'm trying my best not to curse in front of the kids. Rhett is a little parrot and repeats everything I say, much to his mother's eternal annoyance.

"Throughout the years, we've gotten along pretty good, and I can say this without hesitation: I respect him. He's a stand-up guy. A decent brother-in-law. A great leader, and an excellent quarterback. Good enough to win the Super Bowl so he's gotta be all right, you know?"

"Just taking after his old man," Drew says from where he's sitting.

I smile and nod at my father-in-law. "He had big shoes to fill, and look at him. He's already doing it."

"You're not so bad yourself," Drew tells me.

His praise washes over me and I revel in it for a second...

"Isn't this supposed to be about me and Hannah and not you, Bennett?" Jake asks, interrupting my moment.

Yet more laughter and I chuckle too.

"Yeah, yeah, you're right." I smile at them, and Hannah smiles back, absolutely radiant as she sits next to her husband. "I wanted to offer up my congratulations to you both. I feel like I've had a front row seat to your relationship since high school, and you two are a terrific couple. I don't know how Hannah deals with your grumpy ass, Callahan, but we all know she's an angel, so that must be why." I lift my glass in a toast, and pretty much everyone joins in, including the newly wedded couple. "To Jake and Hannah."

"Jake and Hannah," the crowd murmurs as we toast them.

I take a sip of my champagne, glancing over at Diego who's watching me carefully. "I have one more thing I want to share before the best man's speech. Is that okay?"

Diego nods, a closed mouth smile on his face. The crowd goes quiet and I turn my attention to the DJ, who has a remote in his hand. There's a white screen directly behind him and he appears ready to go.

"I had a little video made. Cue it up, bro," I tell the DJ.

He hits the remote button as I settle into my chair and the screen fills with shaking metallic purple pom poms. They pull away, revealing my seventeen-year-old self out on the football field, arrogant as fuck as I start shit-talking to the camera.

All about Jake.

Laughter immediately fills the air, accompanied by a few gasps. Some clapping. The crowd is eating this up. Our friends are howling their approval, and Hayden and Gracie sit up with interest. They've never seen the spectacle I used to make on social media. That was before their time.

There are videos of our rival football games. Footage from the cheer team—Ava shaking her pom poms. And her ass in that cute little skirt. There's homecoming footage with Tony and Sophie wearing their sashes and crowns. Ava and I compiled it all, along with Fable, who was always recording events on her phone. Turns out Ava screen recorded my taunting videos on her phone, and saved them all these years. She swore some of those messages I made weren't just for Jake. They were for her too.

She's right.

"Look at how skinny you are!" Hannah exclaims, hanging on to Jake's arm before she leans her head on his shoulder. Footage of Jake being interviewed by the local news station is playing and Hannah is watching it carefully.

"I didn't know you were going to give a speech," Ava says, her mouth close to my ear. "And I thought you planned on showing this later."

"That was my original plan, but I couldn't wait any longer," I admit. This is my gift to Jake. I know I was a pain in his ass, but watching all that shit I would say to him now, it's funny. It's a good memory. One we can all laugh at because look at us.

We're family.

"Think Diego is mad?" I ask my pretty wife. "I don't want to steal his thunder."

"Babe, he spends so much time with you. He knows how you work." Ava pulls away so our gazes lock. "And look at him. He's enjoying this. Despite the footage of him standing next to Cami Lockhart during the homecoming court ceremony."

Fucking Cami Lockhart. Last I heard she's married to some dumbass and has a couple of kids. I'm sure she puts him through the motions on a daily basis. She was a real piece of work.

"He'll get over that part though," Ava continues, nodding

toward Diego, who's sitting on the other end of the long table the wedding party is at, his wife Jos right next to him.

"Come here," I tell Ava, and she scoots closer to me. I kiss her, letting my lips linger, hoping she can feel how much I love her.

Because I do. I love her so damn much. Hell, I love every single person in this place.

"I have a question," Ava murmurs against my lips.

Anticipation curls through my blood, ready to hear what she has to say. "Give it to me."

"Who is that woman your brother brought with him? She's familiar."

"Oh." I pull away, smiling at her. "Her name is Emily. They went to high school together. They reconnected recently."

A single eyebrow lifts. "Really? Did they date?"

"Kind of? More like they hooked up."

"Maybe she'll make an honest man of him." Ava grabs hold of my arm, leaning her head on my shoulder.

I drop a kiss on her forehead. "Maybe she will."

CHAPTER 16

BECK

I'm leaning back in my chair, watching everyone go out onto the dance floor. Little kids wiggling their bodies to the beat. My mom and dad are out there, and Dad is a terrible dancer. This must be where I get my skills from, ha. Caleb's wife Gracie is dancing and she looks ready to give birth at any second, so I've got my eye on her.

Don't want to see a baby fall out onto the dance floor. Sheesh.

My brother is right in the center of it all with his new wife, and they're dancing to a popular song, both of them mouthing the lyrics as it plays. They've already done all of the formal things that happen at a wedding reception.

The first dance. Cutting the cake. They didn't do the bouquet or garter thing, since most everyone here is coupled off and either married or close to it. And Mom didn't want me or Addie to catch anything because, and I quote, "You're too young for that sort of thing."

She forgets we know all about her and dad getting serious when she was only nineteen. Pretty sure she was married to him by the time she was twenty and having Autumn. I don't want to hear we're too young. Nuh huh.

My parents have no room to talk.

Besides, when you know, you know, am I right? Addie's been it for me since we were in middle school. I turned my crush into a reality and there is no way in hell I'm letting her go. We're attending the University of Washington together. We'll live together too, in an apartment off-campus. We've been looking at locations and plan on going there in a few weeks to hopefully pick out where we'll live.

Can't wait.

Speaking of my girl, she's with her sister right now, sitting with their parents, talking animatedly about God knows what. I could go over there and try to join in on the conversation, but I'm going to let them be. I'll be sneaking into her room later tonight so…

Yeah. I'm bad. But she likes it.

"Bro, what is up?"

I glance up to find my cousin Knox smiling down at me, somehow looking good in a bright Hawaiian print shirt, in a variety of colors, and khakis. On any other guy, it would look cheesy, but somehow, Knox can pull it off.

"Sit down." I incline my head toward the empty chair right next to me. "Let's talk."

He settles in, sprawling his legs wide as he checks out everyone on the dance floor. "This marriage shit is for losers."

I burst out laughing, unable to control myself. "What makes you say that?"

"I know you're all serious with your girl, but come on. We're both way too young to settle down."

"I like being part of a couple." It's true. I really like it. Beck and Addie. Addie and Beck. We just…go together. Perfectly.

"You're a sucker who's too attached to the pussy you're currently pounding," Knox says, narrowing his gaze at me.

He looks like a younger version of his dad—my uncle Owen. Golden brown hair, flashing green eyes, sharp cheekbones and square jaw. Tall and broad just like the rest of us. He's a junior in college and plays football—he's an offensive tight end. He's really good at his position. Could probably go pro.

But he's kind of an asshole sometimes. Not gonna lie.

"That was rude as fuck," I say, keeping my voice even. I'm not going to get angry. Knox is relatively harmless.

I'm really glad he didn't say that in front of Addie though.

"Sorry." He shrugs, not looking sorry at all. "I guess I don't get it."

"I guess you don't."

Addison chooses that moment to approach the table, a big smile on her pretty face as she pushes her hair away from her eyes. "You should come out and dance!"

I slowly shake my head, my gaze never straying from her. She looks hot in that tight blue dress she's wearing. I glance over at my cousin, who's blatantly ogling her. "Knox. This is my girlfriend, Addie."

"Hi." She thrusts her hand out toward Knox, who takes it, giving her the once-over. "We've met before, I think."

"Trust that I would remember you." The flirtatious tone sends me over the edge.

"Hey." He glances over at me, letting go of her hand immediately. "I'm sitting right here."

"Noted." Knox rises to his feet. All six-plus-feet of him. Pretty sure I'm still taller. "I gotta go. We'll catch up later." He nods at me, bows toward Addie…

Then takes the fuck off.

"What was that all about?" She's headed for the seat Knox

just vacated, but I grab her hand, pulling her onto my lap. "I thought you liked Knox."

"I love him. I just don't like it when my cousin is leering at you." I slip my arm around her slender waist and hold her tight. "He needs to keep his eyes to himself."

She laughs, kissing my cheek. "Why would he be interested in me? Isn't he like...twenty?"

"I think he's twenty-one. Doesn't matter. And why wouldn't he be interested in you? Look at you." I scowl, thinking of Knox and the way he looked at Addie. "He needed to stop staring at you."

"Oh, Beck." Addie slings her arms around my neck, her face in mine. "Stop acting all broody. I'm not interested in your jock cousin."

"How did you know he was a jock?" I tighten my arms around her, in case she tries to escape.

"Please. He's got muscles for days." She rolls her eyes, laughing when I glare at her. "Stop. I only care about your muscles."

She whispers that last sentence in my ear. Just for me. And I can't resist.

I kiss her. Right there in the middle of the reception, though no one is paying attention to us. They're all partying it up on the dance floor. Or they're clustered together on the other side of the back yard, closer to the ocean.

Meaning we're pretty much all alone.

I can't stop kissing her. And she can't stop kissing me either. Her fingers dive into my hair, her lips parting, my dick hardening...

"Uncle Beck, what are you doing?"

Addie breaks the kiss first, both of us looking over to find Kenzie standing there, staring at us with those big green eyes of hers.

"Hey, Kenz." I clear my throat, trying to smile at her. "What's up?"

"You've got your hand on Addie's bottom." She points.

My hand drops.

"Daddy does that to Mommy sometimes," she continues.

I wince. Last thing I want to hear about is Eli groping my sister—especially from their daughter. "Where is your daddy?"

"Making bets with Uncle Jake." I love how she just knows exactly what her dad is doing.

"Bets about what?"

"Beck," Addie chastises under her breath. "She won't know—"

"That he'll beat Uncle Jake and go to the Super Bowl next year," Kenzie answers. "Mommy kept yelling it's illegal, but he said double or nothing."

"I'd bet on that," I murmur.

Kenzie's eyes light up. "I'll go tell him! Daddy!" She takes off, screaming for her father. "Uncle Beck wants in on your bet!"

Addie shakes her head, laughing. "Beck."

"What?" I shrug. "She's adorable. It's harmless."

"She talks about hands on bottoms and betting and the Super Bowl. She's too young."

"Kenzie is a Bennett and a Callahan, she'll be fine. Football is in her blood. And there's nothing wrong with a hand on a bottom." I drop mine back onto Addie's ass and give it a squeeze. "We're just being affectionate."

"Right. Keep telling yourself that."

I kiss her neck, my lips lingering, and she sighs. "Let's get out of here."

"Where do you propose we go?"

"Back to my room?" I suggest.

"What if your parents look for us? Or mine?"

"We'll have Kenzie cover for us." That cracks me up, because we both know that little girl will rat us out.

"I don't think that's going to work." Addie touches my cheek. "Let's go dance."

My face falls. "Really?" She nods. "I'm a terrible dancer."

"No one cares. We're just having fun, right?"

Okay yeah. She's got a point.

"Right."

She hops off my lap and grabs my hand, dragging me onto the dance floor. We start to move to the beat, and I'm basically making an ass of myself, but we're with family, so it doesn't matter. I'm dancing with Addie's parents, who have even worse moves, and at one point, Knox joins us, along with his younger sisters Ruby and Blair. They're both close to my age, and we've always gotten along.

They're good dancers, of course. They make me look piti-ful, but I don't care.

Soon, I forget all about wanting to sneak off with my girl. We have plenty of time for that. This is a once in a lifetime experience, celebrating the marriage of my brother and Hannah. It's a big deal.

I scoop Kenzie up into my arms and start dancing with her, making her giggle. All while Addie watches us with adoration in her gaze. I think about us getting married some-day, and I hope it's as fun as tonight.

Nah, I bet our wedding will be even better.

CHAPTER 17

CALEB

"*I* think I ate too much."

I glance over at my beautiful pregnant wife, frowning when I see her expression. She looks miserable, and she can't stop rubbing her belly. "Heartburn?"

"Indigestion, heartburn, all of it." She blows out a long, slow breath, wincing. "Kind of hurts."

"Want me to get you another glass of water?" I'm about to leap out of my chair but she rests her hand over mine, stopping me.

"If I drink any more water, my bladder will explode." She offers me the faintest smile, but it feels edged with pain. I can't wait until she has this baby. Not only am I eager to meet my son, but I'm also ready for my wife to get this over with.

I loved a pregnant Gracie in the early days. She was glowing with health. Didn't really have much morning sickness either. Once she hit the second trimester, she turned into this sex-crazed woman who was jumping me every chance she got, and I definitely didn't protest.

Our sex life was already pretty stellar prior to her getting pregnant. Hell, I'm surprised I didn't knock her up sooner.

"Can I get you anything else? You wanna go back to our room so you can crash out?" I wrap my arm around her shoulders, giving her a squeeze. She leans her head close to mine and I rest my other hand on her stomach. The skin is tight beneath her dress, and I can feel our son is shifting and moving beneath my palm.

Still can't get over that. The fact that there's a little guy in there, growing. Almost ready to come out and meet the world. Life is a trip, man.

More than anything, life is *good.*

The last few days have been epic. Spending time with our friends, some of them we haven't seen in a few years, has been great. Makes me miss the old times. That video Eli put together with Ava and her mom? That made me feel even more nostalgic.

Gracie shakes her head. "I can't sleep lately, so no. Not yet. Let's stay here for a little longer."

"Hey G," Jackson calls from where he's sitting across the table. "You all right?"

She pulls away from me slightly, nodding. "Sort of."

"You look pale," Ellie observes.

The reception has been going for hours, and I think it's finally winding down. The music isn't as loud, though there are still a few people dancing. Some have even called it for the night, though the bride and groom are still here.

"I'll be fine." Gracie waves a hand dismissively, a small cry leaving her at the same exact moment. That waving hand drops to her stomach, pushing mine out of the way and her fingers curl, gathering the fabric of her skirt. "Oh shit. That kind of hurt."

Ellie's gaze flies to mine. "She's not in labor, is she?"

"Hell no." I look around, wishing I could spot Eli. He

swore he'd be streaking through the tables by now, headed for the pool so he could jump in it naked. I really wanted to see that. "That's impossible."

Gracie breathes in and out almost frantically. Like she can't quite catch her breath. "No—way."

Ellie and Jackson share a look before Ellie gets out of her chair and comes over to where we're sitting. She kneels beside Gracie, resting her hand lightly on my wife's arm. "Take deep, even breaths."

Gracie does as Ellie asks until she slowly calms down, then smiles at her friend. "Thanks."

"I think you should go to the hospital." Ellie studies me. "You need to take her."

"What?" Gracie yelps, moving so fast my arm falls from her shoulders. "No. Seriously, I'm fine. It's just Braxton-Hicks."

Ellie frowns. "What's that?"

"Early contractions," I supply. I've learned a lot about pregnancy over the last eight months.

"I think she should go too," Jackson adds. "I understand we don't know dick about pregnancy and labor but, Gracie. You're sitting there grimacing and panting. You look like you're in pain. I wouldn't be surprised if you're going to have a baby soon."

"I am having a baby soon. In three and a half weeks," she announces, just as another agonizing cry leaves her.

Panic races through my veins and I leap to my feet. "Maybe they're right. We should go to the hospital."

"Do you even know where a hospital is on this island? Come on." Gracie shakes her head, stubborn as ever. "I'm not having a baby in Maui. My doctor said I was fine to travel, as long as I took it easy."

I glance over at Jackson and Ellie, mentally telling them, *help a guy out here.*

Jackson gets out of his chair and comes to stand beside me, the both of us hovering behind Gracie, who's still sitting. Clutching her belly and panting softly.

"You're in labor." I brush my hand over her hair, trying to calm her. "Babe. I'm going to get the car."

This time she doesn't protest. She tilts her head back, her glazed eyes meeting mine as she murmurs, "Okay."

I launch into action, heading to our room so I can grab the keys—

Shit. I rode over in a rental car with the others. I don't have any Goddamn keys.

"Hey!" I turn to find Jackson jogging over to me. "What's your plan?"

"I don't have a plan." I throw my hands up into the air, feeling helpless. "I had one at home. I know exactly what I'm supposed to do. There. But here? It wasn't supposed to happen like this."

"Figures your son would do this. Impulsive, just like you." Jackson grins. "I have a rental car. Want me to drive you guys to the hospital?"

Relief hits me at his offer. "Yeah. That would be great. Let me go grab—"

"You don't need anything. We just need to get your wife to a hospital. Ellie's already pulled it up on the maps app. We've got about a thirty-minute drive ahead of us." Jackson's expression turns grim. "Think she can hold out that long?"

"Well damn, I hope so. It's her first baby. I hear it can take a while."

"You took off so fast, you didn't hear her admit to Ellie she's been feeling like this for *hours*."

Shit. "We need to leave."

"I know."

"Let's go."

* * *

THE DRIVE to the hospital was harrowing, thanks to Jackson behind the wheel at a breakneck speed, Ellie constantly telling him to slow down.

I appreciate my friend's lead foot. And that he took over the driving in the first place, so I could sit in the back seat with my wife, offering all the encouragement I can.

She didn't even notice we were going so fast, she's so focused on her breathing. And the contractions. They're getting closer and closer.

Meaning we're definitely having a baby. Maybe even on Jake and Hannah's wedding day.

The moment we pull up to the emergency drive at the hospital, the staff is ushering us inside, a couple of nurses forcing Jackson and Ellie to stay behind while they get Gracie into a wheelchair. We're escorted to a private labor and delivery room, where the nurses get her changed into a hospital gown before they help Gracie onto the bed, with me assisting.

I try to stay out of their way, but I can't help myself. I want to take care of my wife. She needs me.

"Oh God," Gracie groans as we get her situated. "I think my water just broke."

The nurse checks, her brows shooting up. "You're almost fully dilated."

Fuck.

"Really?" Gracie's voice is faint.

"You're at a solid eight. How long have you been in labor?" The nurse's gaze meets mine, and it's faintly accusatory. "Why didn't you bring her in sooner?"

"She didn't tell me. We were at a wedding. We're not even from here." I feel helpless. Dumb. I wish I could take Gracie's pain away. At the very least, ease it for her. I can tell she's struggling. There's sweat around her hairline and her entire body is trembling. "Help her. Please."

"I'll get the doctor," the nurse says before she darts out of the room.

"Caleb." Gracie reaches for me and I take her hand, interlacing her fingers with mine. "I'm scared. I'm not ready. I thought I had a month left. I haven't even packed my hospital bag yet. The baby's room isn't ready either. We were supposed to have the baby shower next week."

"Hey, calm down. It's going to be okay." I can see the panic flaring in her eyes and I bring our linked hands to my mouth, dropping a soft kiss on her knuckles. "I promise. He decided to come a little early, and that's fine. I've got you."

"But we're—"

"Going to have a baby. In Maui. What a story to tell, huh?" I smile, trying to calm my own worry because not gonna lie, this is some scary shit. It's just happening so fast. "Think about it. You're going to be holding our son in your arms in a few minutes."

She rolls her eyes. "Or a few hours. We don't know how long this is going to take."

"It's going to be easy. Couple of pushes and he'll slide right out into my hands." I grin when she snorts.

"Easy for you to say."

"Hey." I lean over her, brushing the damp hair away from her face. I hear the door swing open, a couple of nurses entering our room, but I ignore them. I'm one hundred percent focused on my wife. "I love you. You're strong. And you're going to be a great mama."

Her eyes immediately fill with tears. "You really think so?"

I nod, giving her a soft kiss. "I know it, babe. I know."

CHAPTER 18

ELLIE

*J*ackson is pacing the room they shoved us in while we wait for word from Caleb on Gracie. It's been over an hour, and we have no idea what's going on. Caleb won't respond to my texts, or Jackson's.

He's too focused on his laboring wife, which is what he should be doing, but we are dying to know what's happening. And so is everyone back at the reception. We are getting constant texts asking for baby updates.

"You think she's okay?" Jackson asks me, stopping in the middle of the waiting room, his hands on his hips.

I take him in, admiring his muscular physique, his handsome face. Sometimes it still blows me away, that this man is mine. Oh, we're not even engaged yet, which some of my friends think is troubling, but who cares? Jackson has taught me not to get so hung up on that stuff. We don't need a ring or a marriage certificate to prove to each other that we're together.

We just know. Plus, it helps that we spend almost all of

our time together. We're not even sick of each other yet, and this has been going on for years.

"She's fine. Labor tends to take a long time, especially with your first baby," I reassure him. I remember Ava when she gave birth to Kenzie. It definitely took a while, and I was lucky enough to witness it.

"I can't believe this is happening." Jackson thrusts both of his hands in his hair, slicking it back. He's let it grow long again. It's almost to his shoulders, and while everyone else tells him to cut it, I encourage him to keep the long-haired look. Reminds me of when we were younger, and I had a raging crush on him.

"Me either," I agree. "What did you think of that video Eli shared?"

A soft smile touches Jackson's lips. "It was awesome. Talk about bringing up old memories."

"The videos of Eli shit-talking Jake? Classic." I remember watching those with Ava. I had no idea she saved them all. But back then, I had no idea, at first, she was sneaking around seeing Eli either.

"I tried discouraging him from making those stupid videos." Jackson shakes his head. "But now I'm glad he did. They're hilarious."

"It's been nice, spending so much time with everyone," I admit, my voice soft. "Makes me realize I've missed them all so much."

"Me too." His gaze turns troubled. "Should we stop traveling so much? I don't need to tour as much as I do. Maybe we should settle in somewhere for a while. That way we can stay in closer contact with our friends. Our families."

"I don't want you to give it up. I know you love touring." And I love accompanying him. Life is an adventure with Jackson, and I never want to miss a thing.

"We need a real home base, don't you think? I never did sell that house on the lake," he reminds me.

Shock courses through my blood, rendering me completely still. "Wait a minute. You want to go back home?"

Well, it's not really home for him. He didn't grow up there. Only spent the last few years of high school in our community, and his dad moved out of the area too.

But my parents are there. Caleb and Gracie live there. Jake's parents do too, and Beck is finishing out high school, along with Addie.

"We could hang out there for a while. Six months. A year? I had that one room converted into a studio. I could make music. I need material for a new album," he explains.

I knew this, but I figured we'd return to Los Angeles, and he'd go into the studio there he uses to record. "I love that idea."

"Then let's do it." He grins.

I jump out of my chair and throw myself at him, wrapping him up in the biggest hug. "I love you."

"I love you too." He kisses me, with tongue and everything, right there in the middle of the empty waiting room.

Someone clears their throat mid-kiss, and it's not Jackson. A male someone.

We both reluctantly pull away and turn to find Caleb standing in front of us, exhaustion lining his eyes. A giant smile on his face.

"I'm a dad," is all he says.

We both go to him, wrapping him up in a three-way hug, asking him questions.

"It's a boy, right?"

"What's his name?"

"How much did he weigh?"

"How's Gracie?"

Caleb disentangles himself from us, chuckling as he runs a hand through his hair. "Okay. Let me give you the facts."

Jackson whips out his phone. "I'm ready. So is everyone else back at the compound."

"It's definitely a boy. We already knew that. Silas Jacob Burke weighs nine pounds, three ounces, and he's twenty-one inches. Mom and baby are fine. Gracie pushed him out like a champ. I got to cut the cord. It was awesome." Caleb is beaming.

Jackson pats him on the back. "Congratulations, Dad."

"Jacob?" I lift my brows at the choice of middle name.

"Yeah. Gracie really wanted his middle name to be Richard, which I frickin' hate. The dick jokes I got growing up were endless."

Jackson smothers a laugh at Caleb's glare.

"Why the switch?" I ask.

"In honor of this baby being born on Jake's wedding day. I mean, it fits. Got my kid out of being named Richard." Caleb shrugs. "Jake's always been a good friend to me. No matter what. I thought it fit."

Tears prick the corner of my eyes. "That is the sweetest thing."

Jackson is tapping away at his phone. "I'm letting everyone know he was born. Is that okay?"

"Yeah, that's great. Thanks, man. Shit, I have to call my parents. And Gracie's." Caleb shakes his head, his expression downright wondrous. "I'm a dad."

"Yeah, you are!" Jackson is shouting, and now I'm full-blown crying. "Your kid is trying to one up the reception."

"I think he already did." Caleb seems pleased. "I wasn't trying to steal their thunder, but…"

"Silas totally stole their thunder," I say with a watery laugh, wiping the tears from my eyes. "I'm so happy for you guys."

"Thanks. I need to get back to Gracie." Caleb starts to leave but I call out to him, making him stop.

"Can we see her?" I ask hopefully.

He tilts his head in my direction. "I think I can make that happen. But I'll have to sneak you guys in."

I smile up at Jackson, who slings his arm around my shoulders. "We can't wait to see her. And your baby."

"He's cute."

"I bet," Jackson says.

"Give me a minute. I'll be right back." Caleb dashes off, leaving us alone.

"You want one of those?" When I glance up at Jackson, he explains. "A baby?"

"Not yet. Maybe someday," I admit softly.

He dips his head, his lips brushing mine. "Me too. But only with you."

CHAPTER 19

HANNAH

"*W*ait a minute." We pause in front of the guest house we're staying in, me swaying on my feet, thanks to consuming too much alcohol, and exhaustion trying to settle in.

Nope. Can't be exhausted on my wedding night.

Thank goodness the tall, solid hunk of man flesh standing next to me is my husband. I lean into him, using him as a prop. "Wait a minute for what?" I ask him.

His smile is both sweet and sexy and butterflies swoop in my stomach as I study him. He is so handsome. The bowtie is long gone and there are a few buttons undone on his shirt. He threw the jacket back on before we left the reception and he looks really, really…

Hot.

"I need to carry you over the threshold." He grins.

I roll my eyes. "That's such an antiquated ritual. We really don't need to—oh my God! *Jake!*"

He hauls me into his arms and leans into the door, his elbow hitting the handle and opening it. Kicking it fully open with his foot, he carries me inside. I loop my arms around his neck and hang on for dear life, though I know deep in my heart, he would never drop me.

"I just wanted to show you I can carry you, even with all this on." His gaze roves over the many layers of tulle that make up my skirt. "You look like a cake."

"Is that a compliment?" I arch a brow.

"From me? Yes." He dips his head, his lips finding mine in a quick, soul-searing kiss. "I still can't believe Gracie had her baby."

"Right? We'll have to go see her. And baby Silas." Such a cute name. Silas Jacob, after my husband.

How sweet is that?

"We will. Tomorrow." He chuckles. "Come on, wife. Let's go to bed."

He readjusts his hold on me, making me squeal as he strides down the hall toward our bedroom. We enter the room to find a couple of lamps are on, and the bed is covered in creamy-colored plumeria flowers. There's a bucket of ice on the nightstand with a champagne bottle inside, two glass flutes sitting beside it.

Jake pauses in the doorway. "Who did this?"

"I don't know." He sets me down carefully and I kick off my heels, spotting an envelope on the nearby dresser. I grab the envelope and open it to find a card signed by my new sisters-in-law. "Autumn and Ava put it together."

"Gee, aren't they romantic." His sarcastic tone makes me giggle, and when our gazes meet, I see how dark his eyes have turned.

Swallowing hard, I go completely still. I recognize that look. I've seen it plenty of times over the years.

"Looks like they're pretty romantic to me," I offer, my voice shaky. He makes his way over to me, his stride slow.

Purposeful. Despite his size, he moves with elegance and grace. Almost like he's gliding.

Gliding straight over to me so he can attack me. Cue the dark look in his eyes.

"I've been thinking about this dress all night," he murmurs, his fingers landing lightly on my waist. "And how I'm going to get you out of it."

I dip my head, my hair falling forward, a tiny smile playing on my lips. Oh, this man. I adore him. "Are you up to the challenge?"

"It's going to be a challenge?" His fingers tighten on my waist. "You know I love a good one—and I always win."

"You already won me. I'm not much of a challenge anymore." I tilt my head back, looking at him. "But my dress might be."

"Game on." His fingers wander, drifting over the tulle. The white belt around my waist. He finds the clip and undoes it, removing the belt from my waist and setting it on the dresser. "Where's the zipper on this thing? Or is it buttons?"

"Keep searching," I encourage him, sucking in a breath when he shifts, so he's positioned directly behind me. My head spins when he slides his hands up the back of my arms, his fingers curling around my bare shoulders, and I realize it's not the alcohol or exhaustion that's making me feel off-kilter.

It's him.

His scent envelops me when he dips his head, his hair brushing against my neck when he drops a kiss on my shoulder. "I've been wanting to do this all day."

"Kiss me? You've kissed me a lot today," I remind him, teasing.

"Undress you. That's what I've been looking forward to."

His fingers are now on the back of my dress, searching for that zipper—it's not buttons—but he can't find it.

And I can feel his frustration rippling off of him.

"You're close. Do you want a hint?"

"Hell no," he practically growls. "I'll find it."

He reaches around my left side, his fingers sliding up and down the dress in their quest. When he moves to the right side, I hold my breath, knowing he's so close…

When those assured fingers of his land on the zipper, he murmurs, "Found it."

"Guess you win." I hold my breath when he fumbles with the hook and eye above the zipper, but he undoes it with ease. Of course, he does. "What's your prize?"

"Already got it." He tugs me into him, his mouth on my temple as he whispers, "You're my prize."

There's no more talking. I turn to face him before he can fully undo the zipper and throw my arms around him, my mouth seeking his. We kiss as he undresses me, peeling the dress off of me once the zipper is down, until it falls to my waist, hanging there on my hips. He ends the kiss to shove the dress down, and it lands onto the floor, layers of silk and tulle still up to my knees.

"This is ridiculous," he mutters as he grabs hold of me once more, lifting me up and over the discarded gown, while I squeal in a mixture of delight and fear. I cling to him, my legs going around his waist as he stalks over to the bed and drops me onto my feet beside it. "What should we do about the flower petals everywhere?"

"I don't know—fuck around on them?" I suggest.

His brows lift at my choice of words, I'm sure. "Fuck around?"

Yep, that was it.

I shrug. "Or we could take the cover off the bed."

"Let's do that. I don't want to be kissing you all over your body and end up with a mouthful of plumeria." Before I can say a word, he's leaning over the bed and grabbing the corner of the duvet, whipping it off with a flick of his wrists.

Flower petals scatter everywhere, the cover landing on the ground. While I'm still marveling at the fact that my husband knew that the flowers were plumeria.

I'm impressed.

"You are beautiful," he says, his voice full of reverence as he scans me from head to toe. I sort of forgot I'm still in the sexy bra and panty set I bought just for my wedding day—a strapless bra and skimpy panties in matching sheer white lace.

I prop a hand on my hip, feeling silly, thanks to the alcohol still flowing through my veins. "Should I have walked down the aisle like this?"

"I would've liked it, but I wouldn't want anyone else to see you like this." He puts his hands on me, my skin going hot at his touch. "This belongs to me."

"So territorial," I murmur when he presses his lips to my throat.

"You don't like it?"

I love it. It goes against every feminist thought I have—and I have lots of them, it's not easy being a woman in the art world—but I do love a primal, 'you are my woman,' Jake Callahan.

He wants to take care of me, yet he also knows I'm independent and can do plenty on my own. If it came down to it, I don't *need* him.

But I want him. I love him. I count on him. He's become such a big part of my life that maybe...

Okay, yes. I do need him. More and more every day. And I'm okay with that.

We complement each other. We're partners in this relationship. No one holds more power or sway over the other.

He feels like my equal. He treats me with respect and adoration and love. We share private jokes and we laugh. We share our deepest thoughts and offer each other support no matter what. We get a little wild in bed and there is never any judgment.

More like Jake encourages my wild side.

His hands currently feel as if they are everywhere. All over my body. He reaches for the clasp at the back of my bra, undoing it quickly, and I shed the scrap of lace before I reach for him. Urging him to take off his jacket as I go to the front of his shirt and finish undoing the buttons.

Within seconds, we're mostly naked—me in my panties, Jake in his boxer briefs, and we tumble onto the bed. In each other's arms, hands wandering, mouths fused, tongues tangled. He rolls me over so he's on top of me, his big, hot body lighting me up inside. I run my hands down his back, until they land on his ass, and I push down, trying to get him closer. His thick cock strains against the front of his briefs, and I reach in between us, cupping him there, making him groan.

"I wanted to take my time with you," he whispers against my skin, his hands finding the tops of my panties. "But I'm too impatient."

We help each other strip away the remaining barriers and then he's inside me, buried to the hilt. He goes completely still, his face in mine, and I open my eyes to find him watching me, so much emotion written all over his face, it makes me pause for a moment.

Have I ever seen him look at me like this? Maybe once. Earlier.

During our wedding ceremony.

"This is the happiest day of my life," he says, his voice ringing with sincerity. "I love you so damn much, Hannah."

I cup his cheek, fighting the tears that want to fill my

eyes. They're not sad tears. Not even close. I'm just so overwhelmed with love for this man, I can barely stand it. "I love you too, Jake. I can't believe we're married."

He starts to move, pulling almost all the way out before he slides back in. "Fucking finally."

I can't help it. I burst out laughing.

Finally.

EPILOGUE

FABLE

ots of years later...

It's Thanksgiving. Our favorite holiday of the year.

If you've been on this journey with my husband and me, you know that this was his least favorite holiday when I first met him. Oh, how he hated it. The phoniness of his family. The tragedy that shadowed him everywhere he went. The self-loathing he felt was overwhelming. He was truly the most unhappy boy I'd ever met, but when you looked at him, when you saw the beautiful life he was supposedly living, you'd never think he suffered.

Oh, but he suffered.

I like to believe I changed that. I showed him life was worth living—and he showed me that as well. Our lives made no sense until we came together, and look what we have now.

So much love. So much family that we created. Four kids who are all successful and married with children of their own. My brother and his wife and their three children—who are all married too. There are so many kids running around our house right now, it's kind of frightening.

Fine, it's really frightening, and I'm worried for some of our more valuable objects, but things can be replaced.

Happiness and created memories cannot.

Tired of being in the kitchen and cooking all morning, I make my way to the front porch of our house to find my husband standing there, watching the football game come together out on the lawn. Our son Jake is in charge of making the teams, and he's calling out names, pissing a few people off when he sends them on to opposing teams.

Like Rhett Bennett having to play against his girlfriend. Oh, he does not like that.

My grandson is the spitting image of his father—right down to the attitude.

"Get over yourself," Jake yells at Rhett, which makes my husband chuckle.

"Why aren't you out there playing?" I ask.

Drew whirls around to find me standing there, his smile growing. He's still just as handsome as when I first met him, oh so long ago. A little thinner. Quite a bit of gray in that once dark hair, but that's all right by me. I think he looks distinguished.

I'm still just as blonde—having gone back to the almost platinum look I used to rock in my younger years. Now I keep it that light to help blend the gray.

Good lord, I'm old.

"I'm passing on the torch," Drew says, nodding toward the front yard. "I asked Jake to take over. He's got a better eye than I do."

Jake has started coaching, just like his father. He had a good run with the NFL, and still even has a few endorsements. He's currently coaching his son's football team—they moved back here a few years ago, when the kids were younger, and they realized they wanted them to grow up in a small-town atmosphere versus the city.

Drew and I, of course, approved. They're the only ones who live close of the four children, but that's okay. Everyone is here now. They visit often. It makes my heart full to have my house filled with so many bodies. So much laughter.

So much love.

"You really think he has a better eye?" I ask as I approach my husband.

Drew holds his arm out to me and I settle right into his embrace, snuggling up to his side. "He's younger, so definitely."

My husband has to wear reading glasses now, so this makes me laugh. "He got all that talent from his dad."

"He's better than me."

"Isn't that the way it's supposed to be?" I glance up at him, smiling when his gaze finds mine.

"We did good, didn't we, Fable?" His voice is soft, his gaze warm, and we both turn our heads to stare out at our massive front yard. Nothing but green grass and kids running across it. Our grandchildren. Good-natured arguing and shit-talking from our sons and sons-in-law. My daughters are all in the kitchen, taking over the meal prep completely, and I'm not complaining.

I'd rather stand out on the porch with my husband and enjoy the cold but sunny Thanksgiving Day.

"We did great," I affirm, pressing my cheek against his chest. The steady thump of his heartbeat makes me sigh with contentment. "We've come a long way."

"The longest." He squeezes me tight. "Wouldn't have wanted to take this journey with anyone else."

"I feel the same way."

The front door suddenly bursts open and our granddaughter Kenzie is standing there, looking a mess. Her blonde hair is wild and her green eyes are wide. She's watching the yard with longing, and I know she wants to be out there, playing with everyone else.

But she's the oldest grandchild, the daughter of Ava and Eli. She feels obligated to help with the Thanksgiving dinner.

"You want to play?" Drew asks her.

Kenzie clamps her trembling lips together and nods. "I'm a terrible cook," she admits.

She is a mix of her father and mother, and she's just gorgeous. Smart—and sometimes a smart ass, just like her dad. Fearless. Like both of her parents.

I not only love her, I like her. A lot. She's a joy to talk to. Spend time with.

"Go play. Just because you're a female doesn't mean you have to be stuck in the kitchen all day," I tell her.

"Yeah, who came up with that old-fashioned idea anyway?" Kenzie brushes her hair away from her face, whipping out a hair tie from her jeans pocket and pulling all that blonde hair into a high ponytail. "I'm ready."

Drew releases his hold on me and cups his hands around his mouth, shouting, "Kenzie's joining you guys!"

There is a lot of moaning and groaning, but I can tell even from this distance that Jake is pleased. He claps his hands, pointing to one of the teams. "You're over here, Kenz."

"Not fair!" her brother Rhett yells, along with the rest of his teammates—on the opposing team.

Ha. He knows he's in for it.

They do a coin toss—and Kenzie's team wins. They have the ball and then they do the strangest thing.

Her team votes her as quarterback.

I watch in fasciation as they get into formation and Kenzie gets the ball. Her head is moving whiplash fast, searching for an open player for her to throw to, and when she does, that ball makes a perfect spiral…

And lands in Axel Garcia's hands.

He runs across the grass, everyone yelling their encouragement as he dodges past the opposing team's defense, who can't catch him.

Axel's always been pretty fast.

"Go, go, go!"

"That's my girl!" Eli crows, hopping up and down as Axel takes it into the makeshift end zone.

Just like that, they scored.

Kenzie is beaming as she's tackled by her overjoyed teammates. Her father is literally lifting her up in his arms, going on and on about how great she is.

"Pretty sure Kenzie has the best arm out of all of us," Drew says, his voice tinged with awe.

I laugh. "Right? But she's already in college. She never played football in high school."

"She should've. That's a wasted arm right there. Did you see that spiral? And how far she threw that ball?" Drew shakes his head. "Unbelievable."

Kenzie played lots of sports growing up. Soccer. Volleyball. Basketball. Her true love was softball, and she was so good at it. But she didn't pursue it in college, which we all secretly thought was a mistake.

She has so much natural ability.

"Okay, okay! Let's get back into position!" Jake yells after blowing his whistle.

Yes, our son takes this annual Thanksgiving game very seriously. He even brought his whistle.

"How's dinner coming?" Drew asks me.

"It's in very capable hands," I reassure my husband. "Should be ready around the usual time."

Which is the midafternoon. We have a few hours to go.

"I'm starving now though." He pats his flat stomach. "Any appetizers inside?"

"For you? Most definitely." I frown as he starts for the door. "You sure you don't want to watch your game though?"

His gaze softens as he glances over at the younger generations playing in our yard. "It's not my game anymore, Fable. It's theirs. And I'm okay with it."

I'm suddenly overcome, and he sees it.

He always sees me. I can't hide anything from him.

Drew takes my hand and brings it to his mouth, pressing a kiss to my knuckles. "It's okay. This is how it's supposed to be."

A single tear falls down my cheek, and I shake my head. I'm being silly. "I love you."

"Love you too."

"Forever?" I ask.

I haven't said that in a long time.

"Forever," he confirms.

Guys…I can't let this family go. Now it's the Maguires' turn. Owen Maguire (Fable's brother) has three children, and I'm kicking off a new spinoff series featuring Knox Maguire's story with Playing Hard to Get! Keep reading for a sneak peek!

PLAYING HARD TO GET SNEAK PEEK!

Athletes. They kind of...scare me.

Specifically football players.

There are plenty of reasons why they freak me out. First up is their sheer size. These guys are huge. Massive. Most of them are freakishly tall and overwhelmingly bulky, and when you first see them, they're intimidating.

Second, they're just so dang loud. They enter a building, a room, the quad, the football field (well, that's a given), and everyone notices them. Not only because of who they are, but they deliberately make a scene, like they want the attention. They talk, they yell, they cause a commotion everywhere they go and everyone looks upon them with awe.

And the football players revel in it.

Finally, most of them are extremely good looking. Even if they're not attractive in the traditional sense with a handsome, symmetrical face, the majority of them have a raw magnetism that draws people in—specifically women. There's always a crowd around them, mostly female, though the guys on campus idolize them as well. No matter where they go, they're surrounded. Even mobbed sometimes. It's wild.

I don't get it.

I attend Colorado University and our college football team is made up of the most popular guys on campus. The Golden Eagles are loved. They are revered. When the fall semester starts, they're all anyone talks about: every single conversation, everywhere you turn. The day after their games, where they almost always win?

It's a nonstop analysis of their every move through all four quarters, right down to the final seconds.

All I can ever think is how exhausting it must be, to have so much sitting on their shoulders. They are responsible for the overhyped school spirit on this campus, and when they—heaven forbid—lose, it's like the end of the world is coming.

No joke.

"Did you watch this weekend's game?"

I barely look up as the customer asks the question that's on everyone's tongue this Monday. I work at the campus bookstore, and while I love my job, I don't love these types of questions.

Being truthful gets me attention I don't want. Because I don't watch the game. I never watch the game.

I don't care about sports.

And I really don't like football.

Can't let that get out, though. I'll get my college admission revoked, despite the fact that I've been here two years already and am starting my junior year. I don't understand the adulation, the way these guys are treated like gods on campus when all they do is throw a football on the field.

I honestly don't get it.

"I did watch," I finally answer, lying through my teeth.

"It was a good one, huh." He says it as a statement, not a question. He flat out assumes that I watched it and loved every minute of it. Because…who wouldn't? How could a member of the student body *not* spend their Saturday watching the game?

Glancing up at the guy, I immediately note that he's decent looking, which is…interesting. I haven't really noticed a guy's looks in a while.

He has friendly brown eyes, which are currently zeroed in on my face. His lips are curled into a pleasant smile and he's wearing a Nirvana T-shirt, which is trendy yet also somehow ironic? Maybe? "Can't believe that catch Maguire made in the third quarter," he says.

It takes everything inside me not to roll my eyes.

"I know, right? He's so good," I say, grabbing the Intro to Psychology book the customer is finally getting and scanning it before I add it to the bag of other supplies he's purchasing. We've been in class for a week. Most everyone moved in at least three to four days prior to that. Which begs the question—why is he only picking up this book now? I saw on his order slip that it's been here at the store since before school even started.

The guy scoffs. "*Good?* Major understatement. Maguire is the best tight end out there. Period. He'll go pro next year for sure."

Right. I'm sure he will if this dude says so.

I just don't really give a damn.

"He needs to watch that knee though," he continues. "It might trip him up."

I don't know much about Knox Maguire's knee, but I did overhear a customer at the store say that after he injured it his freshman year, it still gives him trouble.

Like it gave him trouble at Saturday's game. The coaches eventually benched him, but only during the fourth quarter because they knew they were going to win. Which they did.

Naturally.

That I even know these little facts about their first game of the season tells me I retain more facts than I thought I did. And the fact that they occupy even a little bit of space in my brain is seriously so frustrating.

"Yeah, he does need to watch it. You're *so* right." I meet his gaze once again to find him studying me with interest in his eyes. I think I impressed him with the knee talk. I only know this info because of all the chatter I overhear at the store. At the student center. At the lounge in my apartment building that's on campus.

I cannot escape the football players, especially Knox Maguire.

"You like football?" the guy asks, pulling me from my thoughts.

"Sort of." I shrug. Smile. Then hit a button on the register. "That'll be one-hundred-fifty-two dollars and thirty-six cents."

He whistles, pulling his credit card from his battered wallet. "Probably will barely crack the book open all semester."

"Don't forget we buy back textbooks," I remind him, on autopilot.

Working at the student bookstore, I say that a lot.

"I shouldn't even buy it. What's the point? I'll just beg some hot girl to share her notes with me." He taps his card, the reader making a noise, indicating it's going through. "What's your name?"

I don't want to tell him. I don't like this guy. Not really. But I don't want to be a complete bitch either. "Joanna."

"I'm Mark." He smiles.

"Hey Mark." I point at the credit card reader screen. "Mind signing that for me?"

He scribbles his finger across the screen and I stash the

receipt in his bag before handing it over. "Maybe I'll see you around," he says, voice purposely casual.

"Maybe," I echo, knowing I probably won't. He doesn't seem like the type to hang out here or in the library, which is my other favorite haunt. "Thank you. Have a nice day."

"You too." He grins just before he takes his bag and leaves the counter. I watch him go, letting out a small sigh of disappointment as I slowly shake my head.

Men. They're pitiful.

"He was flirting with you."

A startled yelp escapes me and I whirl around to find my coworker, my friend, one of my favorite people in the entire world, Leon, watching me with narrowed eyes.

"You scared me!" I rest my hand against my chest, trying to ease my overly active heart. "And he was not."

"He was," Leon says firmly. "And you were clueless, as usual."

I wasn't that clueless. "What am I supposed to do, offer up my number? Ask him to meet me for coffee sometime?"

"Yes and yes." Leon stands next to me at the counter, nudging his shoulder into mine. I grip the counter, so I don't go toppling. Leon is stronger than he looks. "You need to get back out there. You're moping, and I'm over it."

"I am not moping." I sound defensive.

Guess what? I am defensive.

My boyfriend and I broke up at the beginning of the summer and I was absolutely…devastated. Bryan and I had been together since midway through our senior year in high school, and when we got into different universities, I worried we would end things before they even really started. We were a total high school cliché. After lots of crushing on each other and wasting time, we were finally a couple, only to go our separate ways after graduation.

But Bryan said that it didn't matter where we were. He was in love with me and wanted to keep seeing me, even if we were at different colleges. In different states—he's in Arizona and I'm in Colorado because I wanted to stay closer to home. I, of course, agreed to a long- distance relationship because I felt the same way. I was in love with that boy and fully prepared to go the distance. As time went on, as we made it through one year, and then the next, I felt secure. We were going to make it. Hell, we even talked about getting married and having children, for the love of all that is holy, and then what does he go and do?

Breaks up with me in May—during finals week, the bastard—for a girl named Clara.

She goes to his college. They share the same major. They share a lot of the same classes. Fairly certain he cheated on me with his new girlfriend, though he will deny it until the day he dies.

Whatever. I'm over it.

Mostly.

"You are moping. And it's bringing me down," Leon says, reaching over to pat my hand. I snatch it off the counter, turning my back to him and grabbing a pile of books that need to be put back on the shelves. "Avoiding me isn't going to change things. You're still miserable!"

He calls out the last sentence to me as I walk away, and as discreetly as possible, I give him the finger.

All Leon does is laugh in response. The jerk.

But he's not really a jerk. He's just concerned about me, and I love him for it. Mostly because, deep down, I know he's speaking the truth. I've been especially cranky lately and I need to do something about it. I need to get out of this funk.

How though? I'm not ready to date. Not yet. I'm probably too independent. That's what happens when you're in a long-distance relationship for over two years. You don't spend a lot of time with your significant other, and you learn how to be on your own.

I'm so on my own now, I can't imagine tying myself to someone else. Just...

No, thank you.

I take my sweet time putting away the books, forcing Leon to take over ringing-up duties. With school starting, we've been so busy the last couple of weeks, but it's finally begun to slow down, thank goodness. Despite my occasional grumbling, I really do love my job. I've been here for the last year, and I like being amongst the books and the school merchandise—we are the number-one seller of campus-themed merch, of course. Everyone comes here to purchase their Golden Eagle team gear to wear to football games.

I don't even think I own a single T-shirt with the eagle blazed across it, though I do have a sweatshirt my parents bought me after I got my acceptance email. I still wear it on occasion, but I've definitely never worn it to a football game.

Because I don't go to football games.

Ever.

Like I can't seem to help myself, my thoughts drift to Bryan, and I wonder how he's doing right now. He started college a week before I did and last I saw—after some sneaky social media sleuthing—he's moved into an apartment off-campus with his precious new girlfriend Clara.

Of course he did.

I shove a book onto the shelf, a little more aggressively than necessary, and then turn and run straight into someone.

A very solid, extremely tall someone. It felt like I ran into a brick wall, I hit him so hard.

"Oh hey." A deep, rumbling voice says as he reaches out, grabbing hold of my elbows, steadying me after the blow. "You okay? Sorry about that."

My elbows tingle where the stranger is touching me, and

I shake my head, trying to gather my bearings. "I'm fine." I blink up at him, shock coursing through my blood when I realize who it is.

Knox Maguire himself stands directly in front of me, so close I can smell his cologne, his hands still lightly gripping my arms.

His brows are lowered in concern, his green eyes roaming over me, as if he's checking to make sure I'm all right. "You sure? You ran right into me. You didn't hear me say something?"

He said something to me? "Yeah, no. I didn't know you were standing right there." I try to take a step back, realizing he's still got a hold on me, but then he releases my elbows, allowing me to gain some much-needed space. Standing so close to him is a little overwhelming, but I'm not exactly sure why. "I'm okay, though."

"You promise?" He smiles.

Oh. Shit. He has a nice smile. Straight, white teeth. The faintest dimple denting his right cheek.

"You work here, right?" The smile evaporates, replaced by a no-nonsense expression and tone that tells me he needs some assistance. That's the only reason he said anything to me. Not because he thinks I'm cute or wants to flirt with me, but because I work here.

Not that I want him to think I'm cute. Or want him to flirt with me. Nope. Not interested. Not. At All.

Nodding, I attempt a smile, trying not to act rattled, though that's exactly how I feel.

Shaken. To my very core.

Remember how athletes kind of scare me?

This one is the scariest of them all. He's large and intimidating and handsome and good lord, who allowed a man to smell this good?

"How can I help you?" I ask, shifting into serious customer-service mode.

He scratches his temple, like he's confused, which is still a good look for him. "I need one of those fancy-ass calculators, and I heard you guys still have a few in stock."

"You're right. We do." I tilt my head, contemplating him. "You can just order it on Amazon, you know? For a lot cheaper price."

"You turning away business?" He lifts his brows.

"Just being truthful." I shrug. "And if you have Prime, you should get it fairly fast."

"Yeah, I've got Amazon Prime or whatever, but I uh, need the calculator today." He rubs the back of his neck, seemingly embarrassed. "Class is in two hours. I'm not even close to ready, and the teacher is kind of a hard-ass."

I have a sneaking suspicion who his professor might be and he's right: she's a total hard ass.

"Let me show you where they are." I wave a hand at him to follow, and he falls into step, trailing behind me as I lead him to the other side of the store, where a display of various calculators is located. Taking a deep breath, I remind myself that he's not scary. Not in the least.

I don't know why they intimidate me. The football players. Maybe because they're larger than life? And that sort of thing has always made me want to retreat. I don't like loud or obnoxious people. They put off an energy I find really... draining. And here's where I need to get real.

They remind me of my father. Not my stepdad, who's been the steady male presence in my life the last fifteen years, but my real father. The one who bailed on us and never really bothered trying to see me, especially when I was younger and missing him.

Despite how great Jerry is and how present he's been in

my life, I still feel like there's a hole in my heart my father used to occupy. I know I shouldn't miss him but…

I still do.

He was an athlete. A show-off. A bragger. A car salesman even, though there's nothing wrong with guys who sell cars. My father's problem? He wanted everyone to pay attention to him, including women.

Especially women.

Guys like him. Guys like Knox Maguire, they revel in that. Female adoration.

And I refuse to fall into that trap. My mother did, and she always told me it was one of the biggest regrets of her life.

"Not that I regret having you, sweetie," she always reassures me. "I just wish it hadn't been with your sperm donor."

She can barely call him my father, which I get.

I do.

My gaze returns to Knox as he wanders around the bookstore, sucking up all the oxygen in the building despite its spacious size. Just having him close is making it hard for me to breathe, and I swear I'm not the type to be starstruck.

Yet, here he is, dazzling me with his mere presence.

It's not like he's an actual celebrity, though he's treated like one on campus. Plus, it's his senior year. This is his last hurrah before he's out of here for good. He surely wants to go out on top.

He'll probably do whatever it takes to make that happen.

"Here you go." I stop in front of the more elaborate calculators. The very expensive ones I'm sure he needs. "What class is this for?"

"Statistics." He takes a step forward, grabbing one of the packaged calculators with his large hand and peering at it. His brows shoot up. "Two hundred bucks?"

"I recommended Amazon, remember?" I shrug.

His gaze meets mine, then drifts downward. Like he's checking me out.

What? Why?

"You did," he finally says, his gaze returning to the calculator. "But I don't have a choice. I'll take it."

"You need anything else?" He glances over at me and I try to smile, but I can tell it comes out mangled. "You have all the textbooks you need for your classes?"

"Well, yeah. Class started last week." He says it like, *duh.*

"I had a guy who just bought his Intro to Psychology textbook a few minutes ago." I shrug and start heading for the counter, so I can ring him up.

"That guy sounds like a bonehead," he says, amusement lacing his tone.

I can't help but smile, noticing how Knox keeps up, walking beside me, towering over me. He's well over six feet. Even broader than I thought, standing this close. Yet he moves with almost an easy elegance, which is…weird.

Weirdly attractive.

I go behind the counter, Leon nowhere in sight, leaving me alone with Knox. He doesn't say anything. Just hands over the calculator and I ring it up for him, rattling off the total while he checks his phone. He taps out a quick message and sends it before paying for his purchase.

No words are spoken. No eye contact is made until I offer him a sugary sweet thank you as I hand over the bag.

He takes it from me, his gaze finding mine once more, a barely-there smile on his lips when he says, "You're welcome."

Then he's gone.

An irritated huff leaves me and Leon mysteriously reappears, a curious expression on his face.

"What did superstar Maguire want?"

"He bought a calculator for too much money and then

said 'you're welcome' when, like an idiot, I said 'thank you.'" I shake my head, annoyed. "Why would he do that? Does he actually think he's God's gift to women?"

"Yes, he does," Leon deadpans, making me laugh. "He probably thought you said thank you, like you're grateful to be in his presence."

"Most likely." I glance at the double doors, remembering the flare of interest in Knox's gaze before it disappeared. Like it was never there in the first place.

I read him wrong. Not that I'm interested.

Athletes—football players in particular—aren't my thing.

ACKNOWLEDGEMENTS

I cannot believe this is the end! Can you? I hope you enjoyed this novella, which really is just a love letter to all the characters in this series, as well as The College Years. I'm going to miss everyone so much. I got teary eyed when I wrote the epilogue. It feels very full circle. It's been almost ten years since I self published One Week Girlfriend and now Drew and Fable are grandparents. What is this (fictional) life?

I've already had a couple of people ask for books for the grandchildren (Kenzie Bennett!), and right now is just too soon. But if you've ever asked me about writing a book for someone, you know my motto is, "never say never," because I've written books for people I never, ever planned on writing. And I have zero regrets about all of them!

As you already should know, there is a certain someone who is getting a book because yep, I'm spinning off of this world and focusing on the Maguire kids (Fable's brother's kids) and the first book will be available in the late fall. Fun fact: a fully realized scene came to me months ago featuring Knox Maguire (he is named for his dad's best friend Wade Knox, who has his own book, Safe Bet) and I wrote it so I wouldn't forget. Knox is so obnoxious! And his girl is... not. Ha.

Here's where I thank you for reading my books. And you all deserve a HUGE thank you for continuing to read about the Callahan family and for loving them. I always like to say if you'd told me in late 2012 as I was writing One Week Girlfriend that I'd eventually write about their kids, I would've said, "No freaking way." Yet here we are!

Thank you to my editor Rebecca and proofreader Sarah for helping me slap this book into shape. To Ellie for reminding me I needed Caleb's POV in there. Also to Nina and Rebecca for pushing me to include Eli's POV. I was going to skip him for fear people would be sick of him by now and they were both like, uh no. You can't skip ELI!

p.s. - If you enjoyed **A CALLAHAN WEDDING**, it would mean the world to me if you left a review on the retailer site you bought it from, or on Goodreads. Thank you so much!

ALSO BY MONICA MURPHY

BILLIONAIRE BACHELORS CLUB (REISSUES)

Crave & Torn

Savor & Intoxicated

NEW YOUNG ADULT SERIES

The Liar's Club

KINGS OF CAMPUS

End Game

LANCASTER PREP

Things I Wanted To Say

A Million Kisses in Your Lifetime

Birthday Kisses

Promises We Meant to Keep

I'll Always Be With You

You Said I Was Your Favorite

New Year's Day

Lonely For You Only (a Lancaster novel)

LANCASTER PREP: NEXT GENERATION

All My Kisses for You

THE PLAYERS

Playing Hard to Get

Playing by The Rules

Playing to Win

WEDDED BLISS (LANCASTER)

The Reluctant Bride

The Ruthless Groom

The Reckless Union

The Arranged Marriage boxset

COLLEGE YEARS

The Freshman

The Sophomore

The Junior

The Senior

DATING SERIES

Save The Date

Fake Date

Holidate

Hate to Date You

Rate A Date

Wedding Date

Blind Date

THE CALLAHANS

Close to Me

Falling For Her

Addicted To Him

Meant To Be

Fighting For You

Making Her Mine

A Callahan Wedding

FOREVER YOURS SERIES

You Promised Me Forever

Thinking About You

Nothing Without You

DAMAGED HEARTS SERIES

Her Defiant Heart

His Wasted Heart

Damaged Hearts

FRIENDS SERIES

Just Friends

More Than Friends

Forever

THE NEVER DUET

Never Tear Us Apart

Never Let You Go

THE RULES SERIES

Fair Game

In The Dark

Slow Play

Safe Bet

THE FOWLER SISTERS SERIES

Owning Violet

Stealing Rose

Taming Lily

REVERIE SERIES

His Reverie

Her Destiny

BILLIONAIRE BACHELORS CLUB SERIES

Crave

Torn

Savor

Intoxicated

ONE WEEK GIRLFRIEND SERIES

One Week Girlfriend

Second Chance Boyfriend

Three Broken Promises

Drew + Fable Forever

Four Years Later

Five Days Until You

A Drew + Fable Christmas

STANDALONE YA TITLES

Daring The Bad Boy

Saving It

Pretty Dead Girls

ABOUT THE AUTHOR

Monica Murphy is a New York Times, USA Today and international bestselling author. Her books have been translated in almost a dozen languages and have sold millions of copies worldwide. Both a traditionally published and independently published author, she writes young adult and new adult romance, as well as contemporary romance.

facebook.com/MonicaMurphyAuthor

instagram.com/monicamurphyauthor

bookbub.com/profile/monica-murphy

goodreads.com/monicamurphyauthor

amazon.com/Monica-Murphy/e/B00AVPYIGG

pinterest.com/msmonicamurphy

tiktok.com/@monicamurphyauthor

Printed in Great Britain
by Amazon

44809161R00091